SHETLAND IN THE SHED

"Shona is here," Mandy said. "James and I have been making a little stable for her. She's in the backyard right now. You can come and say hello to her if you like."

Polly's face closed up and her eyes grew dark. For a long moment, she just stared at the table in front of her. Then she stood up.

"I don't want to see her," she said. "I never want to see her again. It was pulling that silly trailer that made us have an accident. Just like Mommy had an accident. I hate horses and I hate Shona!"

Mandy turned to James and saw shock in his eyes. How were they ever going to make Polly see what a wonderful pony she had if she wouldn't even go near her?

Give someone you love a home!
Read about the animals of Animal Ark™

SHETLAND
in the SHED

Ben M. Baglio

Illustrations by Jenny Gregory

Cover illustration by
Mary Ann Lasher

AN
APPLE
PAPERBACK

SCHOLASTIC INC.
New York Toronto London Auckland Sydney
Mexico City New Delhi Hong Kong

ISBN 0-439-23019-5

24 23 22 21 20 19 18   4 5/0

Printed in the U.S.A.   40
First Scholastic printing, March 2001

Special thanks to Helen Magee.
Thanks also to C. J. Hall,
B.Vet.Med., M.R.C.V.S., for reviewing
the veterinary material contained in this book.

™

One

"Easter vacation," Mandy Hope said, smiling as she gazed out of the car window. She shielded her eyes against the bright spring sunshine. The countryside sped past, the green fields sweeping down to the road. Small streams wound their way down the hills, shining like ribbons of silver in the sunlight. "I just *love* school vacations."

Dr. Emily Hope turned to look at her from the passenger seat.

"I wonder why!" she said.

Mandy grinned. "School vacations mean more time to spend with the animals at Animal Ark," she said.

1

Her father laughed. "As if we couldn't guess!" said Dr. Adam Hope. "What are you and James going to do this vacation, I wonder?"

"Oh, we'll think of something," Mandy said.

James Hunter was Mandy's best friend and he cared about animals nearly as much as Mandy did.

"Oh, look!" said Mandy, pointing out of the car window. "There's Prince. Isn't he just the nicest pony you ever saw?"

Dr. Emily turned to look where Mandy was pointing. A brown pony was grazing in a field at the edge of Walton Road.

Dr. Emily smiled as Dr. Adam slowed down a little to let Mandy get a good look at Prince. The pony raised his head and trotted toward the fence that edged the field, his silky brown mane ruffled by his movement.

"He's a beauty," said Dr. Emily.

"Susan is going to the pageant as a knight," said Mandy. "She's going to put a fancy cloth over Prince's back and carry a lance that Ernie Bell is making for her."

"Don't talk to me about the pageant," Dr. Emily said. "Mrs. Ponsonby wants me to go as a medieval lady."

Mandy looked at her mother's long red hair tied back with a scarf.

"You'll look lovely with your hair loose and one of those big pointy hats on," she said.

Dr. Emily smiled. "Mrs. Ponsonby is going as the lady of the manor," she said. "She's just about driven your grandma crazy already."

"She's driving all the ladies at the Women's Club crazy," said Dr. Adam.

Mandy giggled. Mrs. Ponsonby lived in the biggest house in the village. She was the bossiest person Mandy had ever met. Ever since she'd gotten this idea about the Women's Club putting on a medieval pageant, nobody in Welford had gotten any peace.

"What are *you* going as, Dad?" she asked.

Dr. Adam grinned. "Whatever Mrs. Ponsonby tells me to go as," he replied. "Mr. Hardy said he was going as the village innkeeper no matter what Mrs. Ponsonby said."

"Why shouldn't he?" Dr. Emily asked. "After all, he owns the Fox and Goose; he *is* the village innkeeper."

"Mrs. Ponsonby doesn't approve of pubs," Dr. Adam said. Mandy smiled.

"It's for a good cause," Dr. Emily continued. "It's to raise money for the church roof repair fund."

"It'll be fun," Mandy said. "James and I are going as pages. Grandma's making our costumes. But I don't suppose we'll look as good as Susan and Prince."

Susan Collins was in Mandy's class at Walton School. When she first arrived in Welford, she had been really snooty but now she and Mandy were good friends.

"Susan adores Prince, doesn't she?" said Dr. Emily.

"Who wouldn't adore a pony?" Mandy said. "And especially Prince. Oh, Dad, can't we stop for a moment?"

Dr. Adam shook his head. "There's a bad curve just up here," he said. "I wouldn't like to cause an accident. It isn't the best place to stop."

Mandy pushed her fair hair back off her face and twisted around to get a final view of Prince as they passed the field.

"I'll bike over to see him tomorrow," she said.

"And to see Susan, too, I hope," said Dr. Emily.

Mandy grinned. "Of course," she replied.

Both Dr. Adam and Dr. Emily laughed.

"Animals are always more interesting to you than people," Dr. Emily said.

"You should talk," Mandy replied cheerfully as she looked back at her parents.

Her mother's bright red hair blew in the breeze coming in through the open car window and Dr. Adam flashed her one of his lopsided smiles. Dr. Adam and Dr. Emily were both vets in the village of Welford. Their practice was called Animal Ark and the clinic was attached to their old stone cottage. So Mandy, who was hoping to be a vet herself one day, always had lots of animals around her.

The Land Rover rounded the curve that took them into Welford and Dr. Adam put his foot on the brake, slowing the car down.

"Oh, no!" cried Dr. Emily.

"What's the matter?" Mandy said, twisting back around to face the front.

"It looks like there's been an accident," Dr. Adam said.

At the side of the road just beyond the curve, there was an ambulance and a police car. Two paramedics were lowering a man onto a stretcher.

"It doesn't look too bad," Dr. Emily said quickly, reassuring Mandy. "Sergeant Benn is there."

Mandy saw the sturdy figure of Sergeant Benn turn toward them. His face relaxed a little as he recognized the Land Rover and he lifted his arm and waved it toward the side of the road.

"Sergeant Benn is flagging us down," Mandy said.

"You'd better pull in, Adam," said Dr. Emily. "Maybe we can help."

Mandy looked at the other side of the road. A car with a trailer was sitting half in the ditch just on the curve. Sergeant Benn was holding a little girl's hand. She looked about seven years old. Her face was white and streaked with tears.

Dr. Adam stopped the Land Rover and got out.

Sergeant Benn walked up to him, still holding the little girl's hand.

Mandy looked at her. She didn't seem to be injured, but she was very upset.

At once Dr. Emily was out of the Land Rover. "We'll take care of her, won't we, Mandy?" she said.

Mandy nodded. "Of course," she said, looking at the little girl again. She had dark brown hair cut in a bob. Her dark eyes were big with fright.

"I want Daddy," she said, her bottom lip trembling.

Mandy saw the look that passed between Sergeant Benn and her father.

"Is her father the driver?" Dr. Adam asked.

Sergeant Benn nodded. "It looks like he's got a broken leg," he said. "The paramedics have made him comfortable. They're taking him to the hospital. But I need your help."

Dr. Adam looked puzzled. "I'd like to help but I'm a vet, not a doctor," he said.

Sergeant Benn wiped his brow. "I know that," he said. "It isn't the driver I want you to look at. I've got another patient for you."

Dr. Adam looked surprised. Then he nodded and strode over toward the car with Sergeant Benn. Dr.

Emily bent down in front of the little girl and wiped away her tears with a handkerchief.

"The hospital will look after your daddy," she said. "Everything will be all right now. You'll see."

The little girl drew away and looked toward the ambulance.

"I want to go with him," she said, pulling away from Dr. Emily.

Dr. Emily looked quickly at Mandy. "We'll take you to the hospital," she said. "You stay here with Mandy for a moment." Then she hurried across the road toward the ambulance.

Mandy looked at the little girl. "What's your name?" she asked gently.

The girl wiped a tear away, leaving another streak across her cheeks. "Polly Hurst," she said, but her eyes were fixed on the stretcher.

"I'm Mandy Hope," said Mandy. "I live here — in Welford."

Then Dr. Emily was back. She was smiling. "Come and talk to your daddy," she said. "He wants to see you."

Mandy followed as Polly put her hand in Dr. Emily's.

The man lying on the stretcher was very pale, but he smiled as he saw his daughter. "Oh, Daddy," Polly said, kneeling down beside him.

Mr. Hurst ruffled her hair and lifted up her chin. "Now, now," he said, "there's nothing to cry about. I'm fine — really I am." His eyes looked concerned. "You aren't hurt, are you?"

Polly shook her head and Mr. Hurst looked relieved. "They told me you were okay," he said. He shook his head. "I'm sorry I gave you such a fright, love."

"We'd better get you to the hospital," one of the paramedics said.

Mr. Hurst looked up at him worriedly. "What about Polly?" he said.

"I want to go with you!" Polly cried.

Dr. Emily smiled at Mr. Hurst. "We'll bring her," she said. "We'll follow right behind the ambulance." She turned to Mandy. "Go and get your dad, would you, Mandy?" she said.

Mandy turned toward the car and trailer just as Dr. Adam and Sergeant Benn came out from behind it.

"He's coming now," she said to her mother.

Dr. Adam walked swiftly up to them. Then he stopped as he saw the injured man.

"Roddie!" he said. "Roddie Hurst!"

"Oh, my, it's Adam Hope," said Mr. Hurst.

Dr. Emily looked from one to the other. "Do you two know each other?" she asked.

Dr. Adam nodded. "We went to college together," he said. "But we haven't seen each other for years."

Sergeant Benn coughed. "We'd better get Mr. Hurst to the hospital," he said.

Dr. Adam ran a hand through his hair. "Of course," he said. Then he turned to Mr. Hurst. "Look, Roddie, I'll be in touch later at the hospital." He smiled. "I'm a bit busy right now. It looks like I've got a patient of my own."

Mr. Hurst clapped a hand to his head. "Shona!" he said. "I'd forgotten. How is she? Was she injured?"

"Just a bit shaken up," said Dr. Adam. "She doesn't seem to be hurt."

"Thank goodness for that," said Mr. Hurst. "That's good news, isn't it, Polly?"

Polly's eyes darkened and her mouth clamped shut.

"You're glad Shona isn't hurt, aren't you?" said her father.

Polly looked sullen. "I hate her," she said. "It's all her fault."

Dr. Emily was looking worried. "Was somebody else involved in the accident?" she said to her husband.

Dr. Adam looked strangely amused. "You might say so," he said. "Not a human, though."

"An animal!" said Mandy. "Is there an injured animal?"

And before anybody could say anything more, she took off toward the trailer.

Mandy rounded the back of the trailer and stopped. The tailboard was down. Inside was a little pony, tethered to the side rings. She was tan-colored with a long, shaggy coat and dark velvet brown eyes. She wasn't the most elegant pony in the world. In fact, she was as round as a barrel, but that didn't matter to Mandy.

"Oh," said Mandy in a long breath. "A Shetland pony! Isn't she beautiful?"

Very slowly, she approached the tailboard and began to walk up it, talking all the time, soothing the frightened pony. Shona's eyes rolled and she danced a little but Mandy kept on talking in a low voice, stretching out her hand until she touched the pony's rough forelock. She rubbed gently and the pony's eyes grew still. Then Mandy moved up the tailboard and stood beside the pony, whispering in her ear, calming her.

"Well, well," said Sergeant Benn, coming up behind her. "You certainly have a way with animals, Mandy."

Mandy rubbed her hand along the pony's nose and smiled at him. "Isn't she gorgeous?" she said.

Sergeant Benn smiled. "I reckon she is and all," he said. "But that little girl doesn't seem to like her."

Mandy frowned, puzzled. How could anyone not love this little pony?

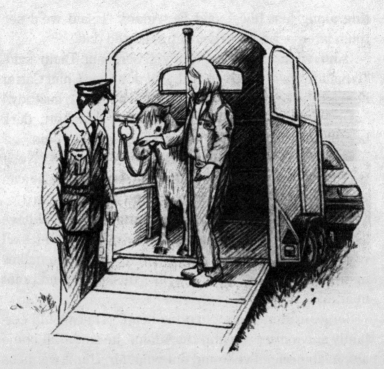

There was the sound of an engine starting and Sergeant Benn looked up. "That's the ambulance going away," he said as Dr. Adam came walking back toward the trailer.

"Your mom is going to the hospital with Polly," Dr. Adam said.

"Is she all right now?" asked Mandy.

"She's still a bit upset, but she and your mom are getting along just fine," said Dr. Adam. "I said we'd see them later — once we get things sorted out."

"And what about the pony?" Sergeant Benn said. "What are we going to do with it? I don't see Chief Carter being too pleased if I take a Shetland pony into custody."

Dr. Adam rubbed his chin, ruffling his short, dark beard. "That's certainly a bit of a problem," he said.

Mandy looked up quickly. "Problem?" she said. "No, it isn't. We'll take her back to Animal Ark. What else can we do?"

Dr. Adam looked at Mandy and grinned. "I might have known," he said. He turned to Sergeant Benn. "If it's all right with you, we'll do as Mandy says. Once she makes up her mind about something like this, there's no point in arguing with her."

Sergeant Benn scratched his head. "That would certainly solve *my* problem, Dr. Adam," he said. "I'll come along later once I've found out what Mr. Hurst wants us to do with the pony."

Dr. Adam looked at Mandy.

"Well, young lady," he said. "How do you like the idea of looking after a pony for a day or two?"

Mandy gave him a dazzling smile. "I like it a lot," she said. She rubbed her head against Shona's shaggy mane. "And, what's more, I'm going to make sure Shona likes it, too."

Two

Dr. Emily had taken the Land Rover to the hospital, but luckily it wasn't far to walk to Animal Ark. Shona seemed pleased to get out of the trailer and into the fresh air. Butterflies fluttered in the wildflowers that lined the road as they left the main street behind. One settled on Shona's nose and the little pony snuffled gently at it.

The noise of the traffic on Walton Road was barely a murmur here. Instead there was the sound of birds, the clip-clopping of Shona's hooves, and the mooing of cows on the other side of the hedge. Mandy saw a small brown animal scuttle across the road about ten yards in front of them and dive into the undergrowth. *A water*

13

rat, she thought, as it ran to the tiny stream that trickled through the ditch beneath the hedge.

"Was Mr. Hurst a very good friend of yours?" Mandy asked her father as she walked the Shetland pony down the road to Animal Ark.

Dr. Adam nodded. "He was," he said. "But we lost touch when we left college. Roddie went on to become a famous show jumper and I became a country vet."

Mandy grinned. "You're famous as well," she said. "In Welford. And you *love* the country."

Dr. Adam ruffled her hair. "On a day like this I do," he said, smiling. "It's a bit different at five o'clock on a winter morning in a cold barn somewhere up on a high hill."

"You even love that," said Mandy.

"Roddie is *really* famous," Dr. Adam said. "Haven't you ever heard of him?"

Mandy wrinkled her nose. "I thought I had heard that name before," she said. "I'll ask Susan. She's bound to know all about him. She wants to be a show jumper herself."

"Well, Roddie's one of the best in the business," said Dr. Adam.

Mandy looked at the little Shetland. "Maybe Polly wants to be a show jumper, too," she said.

But Dr. Adam shook his head. "I'm afraid not," he said. "Polly doesn't like horses."

"Why not?" asked Mandy. "And if she doesn't like horses, why does she have Shona?"

Dr. Adam looked serious. "I had a quick word with Roddie before the ambulance left," he said. "He told me they were just coming back from buying Shona. He thought a gentle little pony would help Polly overcome her fear of horses."

"But why is she frightened in the first place?" asked Mandy, puzzled. "Did she fall off a horse or something?"

Dr. Adam shook his head. "Not Polly," he said. "But her mother was killed in a freak accident. Her horse had a heart attack just as she was jumping a high fence. Polly was only four at the time and she's been afraid of horses ever since."

"Oh," said Mandy, her eyes full of sympathy. She shook her head in concern. "Poor Polly, that's awful."

"So now she doesn't like *any* horses," said Dr. Adam. "Not even little Shetland ponies."

Mandy turned and put her free arm around Shona's neck.

"She couldn't hate Shona," she said. "Just you wait and see. Once she gets to know her, she'll love her."

Dr. Adam smiled. "I hope so, Mandy," he said.

Animal Ark was a low stone cottage with a modern extension housing the clinic attached to it. Mandy rubbed Shona's neck.

"Look, Shona," she said. "Animal Ark. You'll like it here. It's going to be your home for a day or two."

"And that's the next problem," said Dr. Adam. "Where on earth are we going to keep a Shetland pony?"

Mandy thought for a moment. "We could keep her in the shed at the bottom of the yard," she said. She looked at Shona. The little pony's head barely came up to her shoulder. "Shona is so small, she won't take up much room. That shed will be more than big enough."

"And what about food?" said her father.

"I'll get some from Susan," Mandy said. "And I can borrow anything else we need from the Beeches' stables. Susan won't mind."

Dr. Adam laughed. "You've got it all worked out, haven't you?" he said.

Mandy grinned. "Pretty much," she said as she opened the gate.

A head popped out of the clinic window and Mandy waved.

"Hi, Jean!" she called. "Look what we've brought home."

Jean Knox was the receptionist at Animal Ark. Her mouth dropped open in surprise as she watched Mandy leading the Shetland pony up the path and around the side of the house.

"Well, I never," she said as her glasses slipped right

down her nose and bounced on their chain. "Come and see this, Simon."

Simon, the practice nurse, joined Jean at the window. His eyes opened wide as he looked at the pony.

"What now?" he said, running a hand through his fair hair.

"Don't ask, Simon," Dr. Adam said, shaking his head. "Just don't ask."

Mandy settled Shona in the backyard and phoned James with the news of the accident. He was in the class behind her at Walton School. They biked there together every day.

"Poor Mr. Hurst is in the hospital with a broken leg," she finished. "So we've brought Polly home to Animal Ark — with her pony."

"I hope he'll be all right," James said. "Tell me about the pony."

"She's a Shetland pony," Mandy said. "Come and see her. And James, you better wear your oldest clothes. We've got a shed to clean out!"

James groaned. "I might have known there was a catch," he said. "I'll be over right away."

Mandy grinned as she put down the receiver. She could always rely on James. Next, she phoned Susan.

"Roddie Hurst!" Susan yelled into the phone. "He was on the Olympic team. I hope he isn't badly hurt."

"He's got a broken leg," Mandy said. "But I really called you about the pony, Susan. We need some food and some bedding."

Susan promised to get her dad to bring her over with hay and oats as soon as he got home from work.

Mandy had hardly put the phone down when James arrived on his bike, his floppy brown hair hanging down over his eyes as usual. A black Labrador trotted beside him. Blackie was James's Labrador. Mandy had known Blackie since he was just a puppy.

"Blackie!" Mandy called, dropping to her knees.

The Labrador gave a short bark and lolloped up to her, his pink tongue hanging out. Mandy gave him a cuddle; Blackie licked her ear.

"I brought his leash," James said as he got off his bike. "We can tie him up or leave him in the house if you think he might frighten the pony."

"Oh, I don't think he'll frighten Shona," said Mandy. "Let's introduce them."

James shoved his glasses up onto his nose. He looked a little doubtful.

"Blackie isn't exactly the most obedient dog in the world," he said.

"Let's try anyway. Come and meet Shona," said Mandy as she led the way to the backyard. "Then we can get to work."

Mandy pushed open the backyard gate and the pony lifted her head and whinnied. "You've got visitors, Shona," Mandy said.

The pony shook her mane and trotted toward them. "Wow!" said James. "She's terrific!"

Blackie seemed to think Shona was terrific, too.

"Look at the two of them," Mandy said as Blackie trotted up to meet the little Shetland pony.

Shona put her head down and whinnied. Blackie stood a foot away from her, sniffing. Then, slowly, he approached her. Shona stepped forward delicately, her hooves making no sound on the short grass. Blackie backed off slightly but Shona was clearly interested in this new playmate. She shook her head a little and Blackie stepped forward. Shona nudged him and then the two of them were trotting side by side across the yard as if they had known each other for years.

The two animals did a complete circle of the yard, then Blackie ran up to Mandy and James. Shona followed and stopped beside them.

"They're going to be the best of friends," Mandy said with satisfaction.

James grinned. "It looks like it," he said. "I'm really glad I brought Blackie."

"What do you think of Shona?" Mandy said.

"She's so tiny," James said, stroking the pony's rough mane. "I would be afraid to sit on her back."

"Shetland ponies are very strong," Mandy said. "They can easily carry even a grown-up."

"And how's Polly?" James said, changing the subject. "What's she like?"

While they set to work, Mandy told James everything that had happened. It wasn't difficult to convert the old shed at the bottom of the yard into a stall for Shona. Mandy let the little pony wander around the yard while they worked on the shed.

Shona seemed quite happy cropping the grass and exploring her new surroundings. And Blackie seemed quite happy to be with his new friend. Mandy and James worked hard, talking to the pony when she came near. There was no trace of nervousness or fright now. Shona was the most contented pony Mandy had ever seen.

"And you're so gentle," Mandy said as Shona trotted across the grass and poked her head into the shed, whinnying.

She reached out a hand and rubbed the pony's nose.

"We're nearly finished," James said. "Just wait until you see your new home, Shona."

Mandy and James had already emptied everything out of the shed. James piled all the things into a wheelbarrow and Mandy swept the floor of the shed with a long-handled brush.

Shona poked her head farther inside and sneezed. Then she trotted off to the other end of the yard where Blackie was waiting for her.

Mandy swept up her pile of rubbish and looked around the shed. All they needed now was some bedding and a hay net. Luckily, the shed had a half door, so Shona could be warm and snug in her shed and still watch the world outside.

Dr. Adam came around the corner of the house as James finished loading the wheelbarrow.

"That's the last of the rubbish," Mandy said, pointing at the heap of old wood, rusted garden tools, and paint cans that they had cleared out of the shed.

"Your mom will be pleased," Dr. Adam said. "She's been wanting me to clean out this shed for ages."

"Did you hear that, Shona?" Mandy called to the pony. "You're useful already."

"What about me?" joked James.

"Oh, you're always useful," said Mandy. "Are you staying for supper?"

James nodded. "You bet," he said. Then he hesitated. "That is, if it's all right with you, Dr. Adam."

Dr. Adam laughed. "Of course it is, James. Besides, you've certainly worked up an appetite here."

"When do you think Mom will be back?" Mandy asked.

Dr. Adam looked at his watch. "Not for a while yet," he said. "I called the hospital and they're setting Roddie's leg now, but she wants to wait there with Polly until he's all fixed up."

"Can we go around to Grandma and Grandpa's?" Mandy said. "I want to see how our costumes are coming along."

Dr. Adam nodded. "And tell them about Shona?" he asked.

"Of course!" said Mandy.

"Make sure the yard is clear of all the rubbish first," Dr. Adam said.

"We will," said James. "We don't want to leave anything lying around that might hurt Shona."

When they were satisfied that the yard was safe, they biked down the road to Lilac Cottage with Blackie trotting behind.

Mandy's grandpa was in the garden at the back of the cottage, weeding the vegetable patch. Blackie rushed up to him and began to "help."

"Blackie!" James called. "Don't dig there!" But Blackie, as usual, paid no attention.

Grandpa collared him and gave him a pat.

"Hello, you two," he said to Mandy and James. "You look as if you're bursting with news."

"We are," said Mandy. "Where's Grandma?"

Grandpa chuckled. "She's up to her eyebrows in medieval costumes," he said. "I think she's making them for the whole village!"

"Not the *whole* village," said a voice from the back door. "It only seems like that."

Mandy turned to see her grandma standing at the back door with a teapot in her hand.

"Looks like it's time for a break," said Grandpa, putting down his hoe. "Come and tell us your news."

The kitchen table was piled with materials and costumes, so they sat on the back doorstep in the sun. Mandy and James told Grandma and Grandpa all about the accident and about Polly and Shona.

"Poor man," said Grandma. "I hope he'll be all right."

"A broken leg isn't *too* bad," said Mandy, her eyes on the vegetable patch at the bottom of the garden. Grandpa was a great gardener. He had peas and beans and potatoes, cucumbers under frames, and, of course, the black currant bushes that Blackie loved so much. And his greenhouse was a riot of color — geraniums, pansies, hyacinths. You name it, Grandpa grew it!

"So now you've got a pony to look after?" Grandpa said.

"Yes! Oh, Grandpa, you must come and see her," said Mandy. "She's just the sweetest little thing you've ever seen."

"I can understand why Polly doesn't think so," Grandma said. "Her mom's accident must have made her very wary of horses."

Mandy suddenly looked serious. "I would just love to get her to change her mind about Shona," she said.

"That isn't easy," Grandma said. "It's hard to *make* somebody do something they don't want to do, particularly under these sort of circumstances."

Grandpa nodded. "But *you* managed it with Ernie Bell, Dorothy," he said to his wife.

"What?" said James.

Ernie Bell was a retired carpenter. He lived in a tiny cottage behind the Fox and Goose. He was as stubborn as they come, but underneath he had a heart of gold.

"What have you been up to, Grandma?" said Mandy.

"Mrs. Ponsonby upset Ernie by telling him he had to make all the props for the pageant," Grandpa said.

"*Telling* him?" asked James.

Grandpa nodded. "Some people never learn," he said. "Everybody knows you can't *tell* Ernie anything."

"So what happened?" Mandy asked.

"Your grandma calmed him down and now he's not only making all the props she wanted, he's even coming up with ideas of his own!"

"I wondered about him making that lance for Susan," Mandy said. "How did you manage it, Grandma?"

"Oh," said Grandma. "I just hammered a couple of bits of wood together, called it a sword, and told him it was easy, anybody could do it."

James spluttered with laughter. "What did he say?" he asked.

Grandma was trying really hard not to smile. "You don't want to know," she said. "But he ended up telling me that if I wanted to make the Welford pageant a laughingstock, he wasn't going to let me get away with it."

"So he marched off to Fenton's lumberyard, picked

up all the stuff Mrs. Ponsonby had ordered, and took it home," said Grandpa.

"His backyard looks like a Hollywood movie studio," Grandma said. "You should have a look at it."

"We will," said James.

"Grandma, you really are *wicked*," Mandy said.

Grandma grinned. "It worked, though, didn't it?" she said. "Ernie is so interested in carpentry, he just couldn't stay away from it."

"You know, that's what we did when we got him to make that pen for Lucky," said James.

Lucky was a little fox cub Mandy and James had once rescued.

"Mmm," said Mandy. "We've done that sort of thing a few times. I'm just worried that one day, Ernie'll realize what's happening."

"Maybe he realizes already," said Grandma.

"What do you mean?" asked Mandy.

"Just that sometimes people need an excuse — asking or telling doesn't work."

"You mean he really wanted to do it all the time?" said Mandy.

"Of course he did," said Grandpa. "He *loves* carpentry. He's just stubborn."

"You can say that again," said James. "And something tells me Polly is stubborn as well — just like Ernie."

Mandy looked thoughtfully at James. If that was the case, maybe, just maybe they would be able to do something about it. She would have to think about that.

"Now, come and try on your costumes," Grandma said. "I started with yours because they're the easiest. I just need to check the length."

Mandy and James followed her into the kitchen.

"Oh, look at this," Mandy said, holding up a length of dark green velvet. "What's this for, Grandma?"

"I thought I would make caps for you and James from that," said Grandma. "Now, where did I put your costumes?" She rummaged through the pile of material. "Here we are," she said, holding up a rectangle of cloth with a hole in the middle.

Mandy looked at it warily. "What is it?" she said.

"It's a tabard," her grandma said. "You put your head through the hole in the middle and it ties at the sides."

She slipped it over Mandy's head.

"It'll look better when I've put some braiding on it," Grandma said. "And I've made a matching one for you, James."

"But what do we wear underneath?" said Mandy.

"T-shirts and tights," Grandma said, pinning up the hem.

"Tights!" said James. "I'm not wearing *tights*."

"It's only a costume," Mandy said. "Everybody is going to look pretty silly."

"Your grandpa is going as a monk," Grandma said to Mandy. "He and Walter Pickard are going to ring the church bells for the parade."

Grandpa and Walter Pickard were bell-ringers at the village church.

"Just look at my costume," Grandpa said, picking up a long brown garment from a chair.

"I thought that was a blanket," James said.

Grandma laughed. "It used to be," she said. "Now it's a monk's habit."

"You see, James," Mandy said.

"No tights," said James firmly.

Mandy and her grandma looked at each other.

"Stubborn," Grandma said.

Mandy grinned. "You'll have to try the Ernie Bell trick on him," she said.

But James shook his head. "Oh, no," he said. "I know all about that trick. I won't fall for it."

"I'll just have to think of another trick, then," said Mandy.

"No chance!" said James firmly. "Not in a million years."

Mandy only smiled. She'd think of something.

Three

When Mandy and James arrived back at Animal Ark, Simon was just leaving.

"See you tomorrow, Simon," Mandy called.

Simon grinned. "And what are you going to bring home tomorrow?" he asked.

James laughed. "You never know with Mandy," he said as Simon walked on down the path, shaking his head in mock despair.

They found Dr. Emily in the kitchen. Mandy always thought the kitchen was the nicest room in the house. It had oak beams and shining copper pans and bright red gingham curtains at the window.

Polly was sitting at the big wooden table drinking a glass of milk. She looked tired but not upset anymore. She put down the blue-and-white glass and wiped her hand across her mouth.

"Daddy's got a broken leg," she said. "He has to stay in the hospital."

Mandy looked at her mother.

"It's quite a bad fracture," Dr. Emily said as Dr. Adam came in from the clinic. "They've had to put it in traction so he's going to be in the hospital for two weeks."

Dr. Adam raised his eyebrows. "That's bad luck," he said. "I'll take some books over to him after supper."

"Dr. Emily says she'll take me to see him every day," the little girl said. "And the hospital is really nice. They've got toys there."

Dr. Emily pulled her chair back and sat down at the table. She took a deep breath.

"The thing is . . ." she began.

"I take it Polly is staying with us?" Dr. Adam inquired, sitting down and smiling.

Dr. Emily blushed. "It seemed the best thing to do," she said. "Roddie Hurst says they haven't any relatives — only an elderly aunt of his near where they live. Even if she were fit enough to take Polly, it would be too far for Polly to come and visit her dad every day."

Dr. Adam nodded. "And Roddie agrees?" he asked.

Dr. Emily smiled. "He was so relieved," she said. "He's been in touch with Sergeant Benn about the formalities. He's sending a letter to Chief Carter at Walton giving his permission for us to look after Polly while he's in the hospital."

Dr. Adam looked at Polly. "And what do you think, Polly?" he said. "Would you like to stay at Animal Ark with us?"

Polly nodded vigorously. "Dr. Emily says you've got lots of animals here," she said. "Can I see them?"

Dr. Adam smiled. "Of course you can," he said. "Some of them are sick, but we have a hamster who is in to have his nails clipped and a puppy who's here to get his shots."

"And a rabbit with an eye infection that's almost cleared up," Mandy said.

Polly smiled. "Oh, I love rabbits," she said.

"His name is Rory," Mandy said. "I'll show him to you after supper."

Polly's eyes lit up with pleasure. What a difference from the unhappy little girl of only a few hours ago.

"There's another animal here," said James. "One that you know already."

Mandy looked at James. They would have to mention Shona sometime or other. Maybe Polly hadn't meant what she'd said about the accident being Shona's fault.

"That's right," Mandy said. "Shona's here. James and I

have been making a little stable for her. She's in the backyard right now. You can come and say hello to her if you like."

Polly's face closed up and her eyes grew dark. For a long moment, she just stared at the table in front of her. Then she stood up.

"I don't want to see her," she said. "I never want to see her again. It was pulling that silly trailer that made us have an accident. Just like Mommy had an accident. I hate horses and I hate Shona! It's a stupid name and she's a stupid animal!"

Mandy looked at her with concern. She felt really sorry for Polly. The little girl clearly loved animals. It was just that she hated horses — and especially Shona.

Mandy turned to James and saw shock in his eyes, too. How were they ever going to make Polly see what a wonderful pony she had if she wouldn't even go near her?

"Perhaps you'll feel differently tomorrow," Dr. Emily said gently to the little girl.

Polly looked at Dr. Emily, her mouth set in a stubborn line.

"I won't," she said. "I hate ponies. I hate horses. I wish Dad had never bought me a pony."

Mandy heard a car drive up, then a door slam shut.

There was the sound of someone running across the gravel and the kitchen door flew open. It was Susan Collins. Her eyes were bright with excitement and her ponytail flew around her face as she looked around the room.

"Hi!" she said. "I've brought the stuff for the pony. Dad's just taking it out of the car." She looked at Polly. "That must be your pony out there," she said. "Aren't you lucky? She's gorgeous!"

Polly got up, pushing her chair away.

"It's not my pony," she said. "I didn't want it. Why does everybody want me to have a pony? I hate ponies." And with that, she ran out of the room.

Dr. Emily looked at Susan.

"What did I say?" Susan wailed, looking worried.

Dr. Emily shook her head. "Mandy will explain," she said. She looked very worried. "Right now, I'd better go and see what I can do for Polly." She went to comfort the little girl.

"Wow!" Susan said. "Sorry about that."

Mandy shook her head. "It wasn't your fault," she said. "It's just that Polly is afraid of horses. Let's help your dad unload the stuff and I'll explain."

Susan, Mandy, and James went out to the car where Mr. Collins was unloading straw and hay.

"We'll do that," James said to him.

Mr. Collins smiled. "I'll just go in and have a word with your mom, Mandy," he said. "Susan's mom wants to know what color her dress for the pageant is and what kind of headdress she's wearing."

Mandy smiled. "Is Mrs. Collins going as a medieval lady as well?" she asked.

Mr. Collins nodded. "And I've got to wear these legging things," he said. "I'm going to look like a complete idiot."

James looked at him. "You mean tights?" he said.

Mr. Collins looked horrified. "Nobody said anything about tights," he said. He went into the house, looking worried.

Susan laughed. "I can tell Mom is going to have a hard time with Dad over this pageant," she said. "Mrs. Ponsonby is definitely *not* his favorite person at the moment."

"She isn't my favorite person, either," James said gloomily.

"Come on, James," said Mandy. "Let's get Shona's stable organized. You can worry about the tights later."

Mandy explained to Susan about Polly as they carried the straw and the sweet-smelling hay into the backyard. They spread the straw out on the floor of the shed and Mandy raked it.

"Poor kid," Susan said when Mandy had finished. Then she bit her lip. "Look, why don't you bring her over to the Beeches and she can see Prince and watch me ride. Then maybe she'll realize there's nothing to be afraid of."

Mandy and James looked at each other.

"That's an idea," said James. "I mean, it's useless trying to get her to ride Shona. She won't go near her. But if she sees the kind of fun Susan has with Prince, then maybe she'll gain more confidence."

"I'm practicing for the pageant," said Susan. "I'm trying to get Prince used to his caparison."

"His *what*?" asked James.

"It's the cloth he has to wear on his back," Susan explained. "It reaches nearly down to the ground and he's a bit afraid of it. But knights' horses always had caparisons in the olden days."

"Poor Prince," James said. "Even *he* has to get dressed up!"

Mandy hung the hay net up in the shed, her face thoughtful. "Do you think going to visit Prince would work?" she said.

Susan shrugged. "It's worth a try," she replied. "What have we got to lose?"

"Right!" said Mandy. "You're on."

"How about tomorrow?" James said.

Susan nodded as her father came out of Animal Ark, calling to her.

"Got to go," she said. "See you tomorrow!"

Mandy watched Susan race away across the grass.

As she reached the gate, she turned around. "Just wait," she called back. "You'll probably have her riding in the pageant!"

"I wish," said Mandy.

Shona ambled up and laid her head on Mandy's shoulder. Mandy put her arm around the little pony's neck.

"Oh, Shona," she said. "We'll do our best, *really* we will."

The first thing Mandy did the next morning was to go see Shona. Dr. Adam had been to see Mr. Hurst and they'd agreed that Shona and Polly would stay at Animal Ark until he was better.

The little pony was looking well. Mandy fed and watered her and let her out of the shed into the sunshine. Shona kicked up her heels and trotted around the yard, lifting her head to the fresh morning air. It was going to be another beautiful day.

Mandy raked out the top layer of straw and put a new layer down. The shed didn't have to be mucked out every day. Mandy thought once every two days would be enough. Shona trotted up to her.

"How do you like your new home?" Mandy asked, rubbing her face against the Shetland pony's mane.

Shona nuzzled Mandy's shoulder. Then she threw up her head and went trotting off down the yard again. Mandy laughed. It looked as if Shona liked her new home very much.

When Mandy went in for breakfast, Polly wasn't there.

"She's still asleep," Dr. Emily said, setting the table. "I thought I'd let her have a long rest. She was really tired. And then I want to take her into Walton to buy her some clothes. She doesn't have anything except for what she was wearing yesterday."

Mandy nodded. "James is coming over this morning," she said.

"Why don't you both come to Walton with us?" her mother asked.

"Great," said Mandy. "But we promised Susan we'd take Polly over to the Beeches this afternoon."

Dr. Emily nodded. "That should be okay," she said. "We can visit Polly's dad on the way to Walton and you'll have the afternoon free. Maybe your dad could drive you there."

"Terrific," said Mandy.

"What's this?" said Dr. Adam, coming in the back door. He had just been out for his morning run and his hair was tousled.

"James and I want to go over to see Susan this afternoon," Mandy said.

Her mother put a jug of milk on the table and began pouring tea. "And Prince, of course," she said.

"I can take you out there," Dr. Adam said. "I've got to go and have a look at a new bull at Baildon Farm. It's on my way."

"Thanks, Dad," Mandy said.

James arrived just as Mandy was finishing breakfast. Sergeant Benn was with him.

"It's all right," Sergeant Benn joked. "James isn't under arrest. We met at the gate."

Dr. Emily poured a cup of tea for Sergeant Benn and he sat down. "I just came to tell you I've left Mr. Hurst's car and the trailer in the parking lot behind the Fox and Goose," he said. "But I thought I'd better bring along the pony's tack just in case the little girl changes her mind about riding."

Mandy put her chin in her hand. "I don't think she *will* change her mind, Sergeant Benn," she said. "But thanks for bringing the stuff."

"There's a saddle and bridle and some other bits and pieces," Sergeant Benn said. "But I didn't see any grooming kit."

Dr. Emily nodded. "I'll check it out," she said. "We're

going to Walton this morning. I can always get anything we need at the saddler's."

Sergeant Benn finished his tea and rose to go.

"Sergeant Benn," said James, "what are you dressing up as for the pageant?"

Sergeant Benn's eyes twinkled. "I'm going to be the Sheriff of Welford," he said.

James looked surprised. "You mean wear a star badge and stuff?" he said.

Sergeant Benn chuckled. "Not a Wild West sheriff, James," he said. "More like the Sheriff of Nottingham."

"Maybe I could be Robin Hood," James said.

Mandy gave him a shove. "Robin Hood wore tights," she said. "And he didn't have a dog."

James sighed. "I've left Blackie in the yard with Shona," he said.

Mandy looked out of the window. "They look perfectly happy together," she said. "Isn't it amazing the way they took to each other?"

"Where's Polly?" James asked.

"She hasn't come down yet," Mandy said. She looked at her mom. "Do you think Polly will be awake yet?"

Dr. Emily laughed. "Go and see," she said. "But don't wake her if she's still asleep. She had a bad shock yesterday and sleep is the best thing for it."

Mandy went quietly upstairs. Dr. Emily had put Polly in the little spare room next to Mandy's. Very softly, she opened the door. Polly wasn't asleep. She was sitting at the window looking out at the yard.

"Hello, Polly," Mandy said.

Polly turned quickly and smiled. She was wearing a pair of Mandy's pajamas that were much too big for her but she didn't seem to mind.

"Mom is going to take you shopping in Walton this morning," Mandy said. "You can get pajamas that fit."

Polly nodded. "And see Daddy," she said. Then she turned back to the window. "Blackie is nice, isn't he?" she said.

Mandy came and stood beside her. Down in the yard, Blackie and Shona were standing nose to nose. Shona's coat was almost golden in the sunlight. Mandy looked carefully at Polly. She was almost sure Polly was watching Shona. Then Blackie and Shona turned together and trotted off around the yard.

"He's getting along really well with Shona," Mandy said.

Polly blinked. "I like Blackie," she said.

Mandy sighed. If Polly had decided not to even talk about Shona, what could she do?

"How about breakfast?" Mandy asked.

                              *   *   *

The hospital was a long, low building. Its white paint gleamed in the sunshine and the windows were open to the warm breeze. The head nurse came out of her office as they went in. She was a severe-looking woman with neat gray hair and piercing blue eyes. But she was really nice once you got to know her.

"I wonder what she will go to the pageant as," James whispered in Mandy's ear.

Mandy couldn't imagine the head nurse dressed in anything but her dark blue uniform.

"Hello, Dr. Emily," she said. She smiled at Mandy and James. "Have you brought Blackie with you?" she asked.

James grinned. "We left him at Animal Ark," he said.

The nurse raised her eyebrows. "Maybe that's just as well," she said. "Knowing Blackie."

"This is Polly Hurst," Dr. Emily said.

The head nurse bent down and smiled at the little girl. "Your daddy is doing very well," she said. "And he's looking forward to seeing you." She led them down the corridor to the ward. "We're very proud to have such a famous patient," she went on. "And you must be proud of your father, too, Polly."

Polly blushed with pleasure. "Oh, I am," she said, her eyes eagerly searching. Then she saw her father. "Daddy!" she yelled and ran down the ward, throwing herself at the bed at the end.

"Whoa, there!" Mr. Hurst said, stretching out his arms to her.

Polly hopped up on the bed beside him and Mandy looked at the head nurse warily. She could be very strict at times. Maybe she wouldn't approve of people sitting on the beds.

But the nurse was smiling. "Just don't touch that contraption," she said, pointing at a pulley arrangement that held Mr. Hurst's leg straight.

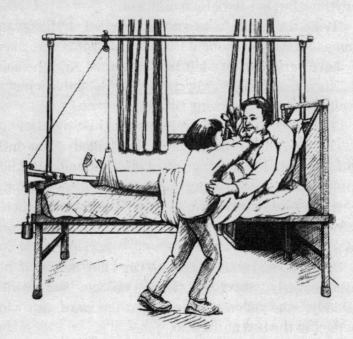

Mr. Hurst looked at the pulley. "Traction," he said ruefully. "Just my luck. But they say it's only for a couple of weeks."

"It must be really uncomfortable," said Mandy.

Mr. Hurst looked a little pale but his eyes glowed with happiness as he gave Polly a hug.

"It's not so bad," he said, looking over Polly's shoulder at Mandy. He turned to her mother. "Emily, I can't begin to thank you and Adam for looking after Polly."

Dr. Emily brushed his thanks aside. "Nonsense, it's a pleasure," she said. "We're just on our way to Walton to buy a few things."

"Like pajamas that fit," said Mandy.

"And some jeans and a sweater and all sorts of things," said Polly, sitting back on the bed.

"A shopping trip," Mr. Hurst said. "Just the thing to cheer you up." He turned to Dr. Emily again. "You must let me know how much all this costs," he said.

Dr. Emily smiled. "We'll sort it out later," she said.

"And I can come and see you every day," Polly interrupted.

Mr. Hurst drew his eyebrows down and looked at her severely. "Just you try missing a day," he joked.

Polly looked shocked. "Oh, I wouldn't," she said. "I won't miss a single day."

Mr. Hurst laughed. "I'm only kidding," he said. "The

Hopes are busy people, you know, Polly. Maybe they won't be able to bring you every day."

But Polly shook her head. "Dr. Emily *promised*," she said.

Dr. Emily laughed. "It's no trouble," she said. "One of us is always passing this way sometime during the day. We'll take Polly along when we're making calls in this direction."

"You mean I can come with you to see the cows and the sheep and all the animals you look after?" asked Polly, twisting around. Her face lit up with excitement.

"You certainly can," said Dr. Emily.

"Wow!" said Polly.

Mandy and James looked at each other.

"She *loves* animals," Mandy whispered to him.

James nodded and shoved his glasses up on his nose. "She didn't mention horses, though," he said.

"How is Shona?" Mr. Hurst said to Polly.

Polly folded her arms. "I don't know," she said. "Mandy and James are looking after her."

"We're going to buy some equipment in Walton," Dr. Emily said quickly. "Sergeant Benn brought the saddle and bridle over but there are a few things we need."

"Currycombs and brushes," said Mr. Hurst. "I didn't bother to buy those for Shona. We've got plenty at home. But I had to get a properly fitting saddle and bridle for her. Where are you going to go?"

Dr. Emily began talking about the saddler's in Walton and Mandy saw Mr. Hurst's face light up with interest. *What a pity Polly couldn't share his enthusiasm,* thought Mandy. *Polly loves animals so much! If only she could get over her fear of Shona, she would love her pony, too.* Mandy was sure of it. But that would take a miracle, and Mandy didn't think she could manage to produce a miracle!

Four

"Just the saddler's now," said Dr. Emily as they walked along Walton High Street.

Polly looked sideways at her but didn't say anything. They were loaded down with bags. Polly had really enjoyed her shopping trip.

Dr. Emily looked at Polly. "Then we'll have some ice cream."

Polly smiled.

The saddler's smelled wonderful to Mandy. The smell of leather mingled with polish and oil. There were saddles arranged all around the walls and bits of bridles and reins and boots — everything you could possible need for a pony.

"Brushes," said Dr. Emily, making for a display on the far wall.

Mr. Todd, the saddler, came out of the back of the shop. He peered at them over his half-moon glasses. He had a long curved needle in one hand and a bridle in the other.

"Just doing some repairs," he said. "Well, Dr. Emily, what can I do for you?"

Dr. Emily explained while Mandy and James poked around the shelves.

"What's this?" said James, holding up a brush with a metal hook at one end.

"That hook is a hoof pick," said Polly.

"But what about the brush?" James asked.

Mandy opened her mouth to explain, then bit the words back. Polly took the hoof pick in her hands. It was a much better idea to let Polly tell James.

"You clean the underneath of the horse's hooves with this part," said Polly, pointing to the hook. "Then you can brush any dirt away with the brush."

Dr. Emily was holding up a brush. "What about this one?" she said to Mr. Todd. "We need a body brush."

Polly turned quickly. "Oh, no, not that one," she said.

"You can't buy that. Shetlands have very rough coats. You need one with longer bristles."

Dr. Emily looked at her in surprise.

"Oh," she said. "What kind do you think we need, Polly?"

Mandy cast a quick look at James as Polly walked across the shop to look at Mr. Todd's array of brushes.

She picked one up. "Maybe this one," she said to Mr. Todd.

"For a Shetland pony?" he said to her. "Now, you're right about having a good stiff brush but what about a dandy brush?"

"Yes — and we'll need currycombs as well," Polly said, frowning over the two brushes. "A rubber one and a metal one for cleaning the brushes."

Mr. Todd's eyes twinkled behind his glasses. "Well, Dr. Emily, you've certainly got an expert here," he said.

Dr. Emily looked bemused. "So I see," she said. "I think we'll leave it up to Polly. She seems to know what she's doing."

Mandy and James looked at each other as Polly and Mr. Todd talked away about brushes and currycombs.

"She might not like horses," said James, "but she certainly knows a lot about them."

Mandy nodded thoughtfully. "And she's really interested," she said. "Just listen to her. You know, James, that could be useful."

"What do you mean?" said James.

Polly was completely engrossed in choosing the brushes.

"I think I've just had an idea," said Mandy. She drew James to the far end of the shop.

"Remember what Grandma and Grandpa were saying about getting Ernie Bell to do things?" she asked.

James nodded. "Things he doesn't want to do," he said.

Mandy frowned thoughtfully. "Maybe not," she said. "Grandma and Grandpa thought it was just stubbornness. That Ernie really wanted to do the things — deep down."

"So?" said James.

"I think perhaps Polly's like that," she said. "I think she really *is* interested in horses. I mean, she knows all about them. Just look at her."

Polly was testing a brush with her fingers, feeling the bristles.

"She's really interested in those brushes," said James. "But that doesn't mean she *likes* horses."

"Maybe not," said Mandy. "But I caught her looking out of her bedroom window this morning. Polly tried to make me think she was looking at Blackie but I don't know. I think she was watching Shona. I think deep down she really does like horses."

"But she's afraid of them," said James.

"Maybe," said Mandy. "But maybe it's like I said. Maybe she doesn't *want* to like them."

"Okay," said James. "But even if you're right, what do we do about it? And what's Ernie Bell got to do with it?"

Mandy looked thoughtful. "What if I ask Susan to act as if she doesn't know how to look after Prince this afternoon? Ask her to groom him wrongly or something," she said.

"What good would that do?" said James. Then he stopped. "You mean, if Polly saw that Susan was doing it wrong, she'd say so?" he said.

"Maybe she'd even do it herself," said Mandy. "Like Ernie Bell."

"Or like choosing the brushes," James said. "You might be right, Mandy."

"It's worth a try," said Mandy.

"But would Susan play along?" James asked.

"I *think* so," Mandy said. "So long as I didn't ask her to do anything that would really upset Prince."

"And why Prince?" said James. "I mean, why couldn't we do the same thing with Shona?"

Mandy frowned. "Because Polly doesn't want to get

near Shona," she said. "I think she doesn't want to let herself like her. With Susan's horse, it's different. It isn't her own pony."

"So you think she really *does* like Shona?"

Mandy thought for a moment. "Yes," she said.

"Then let's try it," said James. "It's silly if she has a pony she secretly likes and won't go near!"

Dr. Emily had to make a call on the way back to Animal Ark.

"Ernie Bell's cat, Twinkie, has a sore paw," she said. "I promised I'd look in on him this morning."

"We can have a look at all the things he's made for the pageant," James said.

"And you can meet Sammy," Mandy said to Polly.

"Who's Sammy?" Polly asked.

"A squirrel," Mandy replied. "Ernie adopted him. He was an orphan and Ernie made him a terrific run in the backyard. You'll love Sammy."

Polly squirmed with excitement. She really did love animals.

"Here we are," said Dr. Emily as they drew up in front of the row of cottages behind the Fox and Goose.

Ernie was waiting for them. He was an old man with a wrinkled, weather-beaten face and grizzly gray hair. He was holding Twinkie in his arms.

"Poor Twinkie," said Mandy, tickling the cat under the chin.

Twinkie blinked at her and licked his paw.

Dr. Emily looked at it. "It seems to be infected, Ernie," she said. "Let's get him inside and I'll examine it properly."

Ernie turned back inside. "I suppose you'll want to see Sammy?" he said to Mandy and James. Then he looked at Polly. "And who's this?"

Mandy introduced Polly. "Her father is a famous show jumper," Mandy finished.

"Hmmph," grunted Ernie, unimpressed. "You'll find a bag of nuts on the kitchen counter," he said gruffly. "And make sure you don't touch anything for the pageant."

"Thanks, Mr. Bell," Mandy said as the three of them raced through the little cottage and into the backyard. Mandy picked up the nuts on the way.

"Wow!" said James, looking around the yard. "Your grandma was right. It *does* look like a movie studio."

The yard seemed to be filled with funny-shaped bits of wood. They really did look like bits of scenery. They were propped against the back wall of the cottage, against the fence at the bottom of the yard, and even against Sammy's run.

"What do you think this is?" said James.

Mandy looked where James was pointing. There was a kind of platform arrangement with a turret and flagpole on top.

"That must be Mrs. Ponsonby's castle," Mandy said.

James laughed. "You're kidding!" he said. "She hasn't actually got Ernie making a castle?"

Mandy shrugged. "She said she wanted some kind of platform for speeches," she said.

"Mrs. Ponsonby is making a speech?" James groaned. "It'll go on forever."

But Mandy wasn't listening. She was off, running toward Sammy's pen. "I've brought somebody new to see you, Sammy," she said, poking her fingers through the wire mesh.

The little gray squirrel looked up at her with bright eyes and scrambled up the netting.

"Oh, isn't he lovely?" said Polly. "Can't we take him out?"

Mandy looked at her. Her eyes were shining as she looked at the little animal.

"We can ask Ernie when Mom has finished treating Twinkie," Mandy said. "Sometimes Ernie walks around with Sammy on his shoulder."

"Oh, I'd love to do that," Polly said. "Oh, look at Sammy running around!"

Sammy's pen was big enough for even the most active squirrel. There was a long run for him to scamper around in and plenty of posts and the wire netting for him to climb.

"Would you like to feed him?" Mandy asked.

Polly nodded eagerly and Mandy poured some nuts into her hand.

Polly was delighted. Sammy bounded toward her and took a nut from her hand. He held it delicately between his little paws and nibbled on it.

"Oh, he's so cute," said Polly. "Look at him!"

But Mandy was looking at Polly instead. She was having a wonderful time.

By the time Dr. Emily and Ernie Bell came out of the cottage, all the nuts were gone.

"How's Twinkie?" asked Mandy at once.

Dr. Emily smiled. "Fine," she said. "The paw was infected so I had to put some antibiotic cream on it and bandage it."

"I bet Twinkie *loved* that," said James.

Dr. Emily laughed. "He put up quite a fight," she said. "But Ernie and I managed. The paw should be all right in a day or two. Let's hope the bandage stays on."

"I'll see that it does," Ernie said.

Polly tugged at Mandy's sleeve. "What about Sammy?" she whispered.

Mandy smiled at her. "Can we take Sammy out of the

pen, Mr. Bell?" she asked. "Polly would love to hold him."

Ernie Bell scratched his chin. "I don't see why not," he said, reaching for the catch on the door of the pen.

Sammy came to him at once and Ernie picked up the little squirrel and handed him to Polly.

"Careful, now," he said. "Don't hold him too tightly."

"Oh, I won't," Polly breathed, cradling Sammy. "Oh, thank you, Mr. Bell."

"Mr. Bell," James said, "is that really Mrs. Ponsonby's castle?"

Ernie Bell looked as if he wanted to tell them exactly what he thought of Mrs. Ponsonby's castle.

"Come and see the rest of the things," he said. And he and James went wandering off down the yard.

"Sammy seems very happy with you, Polly," Dr. Emily said. "You must like animals a lot."

"Oh, I do," said Polly, her face flushed with happiness.

"Is Twinkie really all right?" Mandy asked her mother anxiously.

"Of course," Dr. Emily said. "Don't worry. It's only a mild infection. He must have cut his paw digging in the garden and it got infected." She looked at James and Ernie. "If we want to get back for lunch, we'd better get going," she said. "It's been a busy morning."

It certainly had, thought Mandy. And she still had to phone Susan.

"James!" she called. "Time to go."

James and Ernie came back up the yard. Polly handed Sammy back to Ernie.

"You've done such a lot of work for the pageant, Ernie," Dr. Emily said.

Ernie flushed with pleasure. "Somebody had to do it," he said. "And you can't have amateurs tackling a job like this. If you want a job done well, do it yourself. That's my motto."

"It's great that you enjoy it so much," Mandy said innocently and James gave her a look.

"I wouldn't do it otherwise," said Ernie, putting Sammy back in the pen and latching the door. "Nobody makes Ernie Bell do what he doesn't want to do."

Polly was looking at him intently. "People try to make me do things I don't want to do," she said.

Ernie Bell looked at her. "Don't let them," he said. "Stick to your guns."

Mandy's heart sank. In the case of Shona, she didn't want Polly to "stick to her guns."

"Mr. Bell, what are you dressing up as for the pageant?" James said.

Mandy looked at James. She could tell he was longing to ask Ernie if *he* was going to wear tights but didn't dare.

"Dressing up?" Ernie said. "You won't catch me dressing up. I'm going as a carpenter because that's what I am. And, what's more, I'm going in my own clothes."

Mandy looked at Ernie standing there in a shapeless canvas shirt and a worn pair of corduroy trousers tucked into his boots. Dressed like that, he certainly wouldn't be out of place at a medieval pageant. He looked as if he'd stepped straight out of an old-fashioned painting.

"Time to go," Dr. Emily said firmly. "A vet's life is a busy one. I've got office hours after lunch."

Mandy didn't get the chance to phone Susan until after lunch when Polly had gone upstairs to change into her new clothes. She knew she was asking a very big favor.

"What?" exclaimed Susan. "I can't do that!"

"Yes, you can," said Mandy. "Honestly, I'm sure it'll work."

"But I don't know if I could keep it up," Susan said.

Mandy heard Polly running downstairs and out the front door.

"Just try it, Susan," Mandy pleaded. "Promise?"

"Oh, I'll try it," said Susan. "But I don't know what Prince will think."

Mandy put the phone down just as her dad came into the room.

"Ready?" he said. "Polly and James are in the car."

"Ready," Mandy agreed.

"Let's go, then," said her dad. Then he looked closely at her. "What are you up to, Mandy Hope?"

"Up to?" Mandy said innocently. "Why should I be up to anything?"

"Because you've got that look in your eye that tells me you're hatching a plot," Dr. Adam said, grinning. Then he sighed. "Still, I suppose it's better if I don't know. After all, I'm getting old. I can't take too many surprises."

Mandy laughed and gave her dad a push. "Mom says you're as fit as a fiddle with all your jogging and the exercise bike and stuff," she said.

Dr. Adam looked interested. "Aha!" he said as they went out to the car. "I must remember that the next time she tells me I'm eating too many chips."

Dr. Adam dropped them off at the Beeches. The Beeches was a massive modern ranch house set in its own grounds on the Walton to Welford road. The paddock came right down to the road in front of the house. It had a whole stable block at the back of it. Mandy, Polly, and James went straight around to the back.

"Hi!" said Susan, coming around the corner of the stables. She gave Mandy an anxious look. "I've just got a couple of things to do."

"We'll come and watch," Mandy said quickly, and James gave her a look.

Susan led them around to the stables. Prince poked his head out of his stall and whinnied as he saw them.

"Hello there, Prince," said Mandy, reaching up to him. "How are you, boy?"

Prince whinnied and turned his head to blow on Mandy's cheek. Mandy rubbed his nose and the pony whinnied again as if to say hello.

"He needs a good brushing," Susan said awkwardly.

"You go ahead, Susan," Mandy said. "We'll just watch, won't we, Polly?"

Polly looked warily at Prince and took a step back. "If you like," she said.

Susan opened the stall door and stepped inside. She picked up a brush and began to groom Prince in quick, jerky movements. Mandy cast a sideways glance at Polly. She was staring at Susan, her lips pursed.

Prince shook his head and looked around at Susan with a reproachful eye. Poor Susan kept on jerking the brush across his gleaming coat, ruffling it.

Mandy looked at Polly again. The little girl was almost dancing with impatience.

"That's not the way you do it!" she finally burst out, unable to stop herself.

Susan looked at her and drew herself up. "It's the way *I* do it," she said.

Good for you, Susan, Mandy said to herself.

"Poor Prince," James whispered in her ear.

Prince was shaking his head now and making little dancing steps. Mandy drew James back out of earshot of Polly.

"Do you think this is going to work?" said James, looking at Polly.

The little girl was standing absolutely still, looking at Susan and Prince.

"Let's just wait and see," Mandy said, and crossed her fingers.

Polly moved closer to Susan. "You've got to do it smoothly," she said. "You're all jerky. You'll upset him."

Susan shook her ponytail. "What do you know about it?" she said. "I've had Prince for ages."

"I've got a pony, too," said Polly.

Mandy held her breath. Polly had actually called Shona *her* pony.

Polly bit her lip.

"But you don't take care of her," said Susan.

"Maybe I don't," said Polly. "But at least I know *how* to. I've watched Daddy hundreds of times."

Susan paused, looking at the little girl. Mandy thought her friend was doing really well.

"Okay, then. If you know so much, maybe you can show me," she said.

But Polly still didn't move. Her eyes went from Susan to Prince. She stood there for a long moment and Mandy chewed her lip. Would she fall for it? Then Polly marched forward and stood beside the pony. She took the brush from Susan's hand.

"You do it like this," she said, moving the brush in long sweeping strokes over Prince's flanks. "This is the way Daddy always does it."

Susan looked over Polly's head at Mandy.

"Okay?" she mouthed.

Mandy beamed at her. She nodded and gave a thumbs-up sign.

Prince turned his head and looked at the little girl grooming him.

"Good boy," Polly said softly, and Prince whinnied back.

"She's a natural," said Mandy to James. "Just look at her. Prince adores her. She's perfect with him."

"No wonder," said James. "I mean it's in her blood, isn't it? I don't suppose you can have an international show jumper for a dad and not have a talent for horses."

Mandy looked at Polly again. She was lost in her

work, following the brush with her eyes, murmuring to Prince all the while.

"She must have watched Mr. Hurst do this hundreds of times," James said.

Then Polly seemed to realize what she was doing. She stood back and handed the brush to Susan. "That's how you do it," she said gruffly, and walked out of the stall.

Mandy smiled at her. "You really do know how to look after horses, don't you, Polly?" she asked.

Polly shrugged. "Anybody can learn to look after horses," she said. "It doesn't mean you have to *like* them."

Mandy looked at James. They'd made a start, but they still had a long way to go.

Five

Mandy made sure they dropped in at the Beeches the following day. It was on the way to the hospital, and Susan was a good friend.

After that visit, Mandy had the feeling that Polly was beginning to enjoy herself — especially after she had watched Susan trying out Prince's caparison.

It was a bit like a horse blanket but much longer and of a lighter material. Susan had used an old brocade curtain. It was deep blue and looked wonderful against Prince's gleaming brown coat.

"Oh, doesn't he look nice?" Polly said.

Mandy nodded. Prince looked really elegant. Susan seemed a bit odd perched on top of such a beautifully dressed pony in her old jeans and sweater.

"It'll look much better when I'm dressed up, too," Susan said.

She wheeled Prince around and began to walk him down the yard to the lush green grass of the paddock.

Mandy and Polly stood under a tall oak tree at the entrance to the paddock, watching her put Prince through his paces. High above them the wind murmured in the tree, the rustling of its leaves mingling with birdsong.

"Susan is a really good rider, isn't she?" the little girl said to Mandy.

"She's terrific," Mandy said. "It can't be easy riding Prince with that on his back."

Susan eased Prince into a gentle trot. The caparison fluttered around his legs and he shied slightly. Susan laid a hand on his neck, soothing him, reassuring him. Prince settled down. Mandy could see he would soon get used to the strange feeling of cloth flapping around his legs.

"And she's really good at grooming him now," said Polly. "Since I showed her how."

Mandy looked down at her quickly, but Polly obviously had no suspicion that she had been tricked.

Mandy smiled. Susan had been a very quick learner, indeed.

It was strange, Mandy thought. *Polly would stand quite close to Prince now and even pat him, but she still wouldn't go near Shona.* Mandy was beginning to lose hope. Maybe Polly would *never* let herself like Shona. She still seemed to blame the pony for the accident on Walton Road.

But the next day, Mandy got a pleasant surprise. She and James were on their way out to the backyard to check Shona's food when she suddenly stopped.

"Look!" Mandy said to James.

"What?" said James, coming to stand beside her at the back door of Animal Ark.

"Polly is out in the yard with Blackie and Shona," Mandy said.

"She loves Blackie," James said.

Mandy nodded. "I know that," she replied. "She's always out there when Blackie is around. But I think she wants to make friends with Shona at last. I think she's making friends through Blackie."

"What do you mean?" said James, puzzled.

"Watch Polly," Mandy said softly.

James looked down the yard to where Polly was patting Blackie. Shona kept looking over toward her. Then

Shona lifted her head and trotted toward the little girl. Polly got up quickly and moved back as the pony slowed to a walk and stopped just in front of her.

Blackie looked up at the pony and Shona put her head down and butted him gently on the nose. Blackie butted her back.

"Those two are the best of friends," James said, watching Shona and Blackie.

But Mandy's eyes were on Polly.

"Watch," she said softly.

Polly moved toward Shona and Blackie and put out her hand to stroke Blackie's head. The pony lifted her head and moved it toward Polly's hand. Mandy held her breath. For a moment she thought Polly was going to pull her hand away, but she left it where it was, resting on Blackie's head.

Shona opened her lips and nuzzled Polly's hand. Still the little girl didn't pull away, but let the pony taste her fingers. Then she put out her other hand and touched Shona softly on the neck. Shona moved her head under Polly's hand and Polly began to stroke her rough nose.

"Wow!" said James. "She *is* getting to like Shona."

Mandy nodded. "She's still nervous around her," she said. "But once she learns how gentle Shona is, she'll be more confident. All she needs is time."

Just then there was the sound of a car engine, then a door slamming. A figure appeared around the side of the house — a large woman with a flowery hat and pink-rimmed spectacles. She had a Pekingese under one arm. Another dog, a scruffy one, danced around her feet, barking.

It was Mrs. Ponsonby with her dogs, Pandora and Toby.

"Coo-eee!" Mrs. Ponsonby called. Then she caught sight of Polly in the yard. She leaned on the gate and beamed at her. "You must be Polly," she said. "Now, isn't that a lovely pony? Are you going to be a show jumper just like your father?"

Mandy gasped. Trust Mrs. Ponsonby to put her foot in it!

Polly's hand shot away from the pony and she looked at Mrs. Ponsonby. Shona, alarmed by the sudden noise, kicked up her heels and went galloping across the grass, swishing her tail. The end of the little pony's tail caught Polly sharply across the cheek and she put her hand up to her face. She had become pale.

Then she turned and ran toward the back door, barging past Mandy and James and disappearing into the kitchen.

"Oh, Mrs. Ponsonby!" Mandy said in despair.

"Now, what was that all about?" said Mrs. Ponsonby, pushing open the gate.

Toby rushed toward Mandy and James, barking his head off, and Pandora squirmed her way out of Mrs. Ponsonby's arms and thudded onto the ground. She shook herself and ran, yapping, after Toby.

"That little girl must be very shy," said Mrs. Ponsonby, marching toward them. "She'll have to get over that if she wants to be a champion show jumper."

"Hello, Mrs. Ponsonby," James said, and immediately bent down to Toby, who was trying to crawl up his legs.

"She doesn't want to be a show jumper," Mandy said.

Mrs. Ponsonby looked at her. "Don't be silly, Mandy," she said. "With a father who was on the Olympic team? Of *course* she wants to be a show jumper! Now, where's your mother? I want to talk to her about the pageant. And I want her to get Roddie Hurst to give a talk to the Women's Club. The ladies are all *thrilled* to have such a celebrity on our doorstep." She bent closer to Mandy. "And I hear your father is an old friend of his," she said, wagging a finger at Mandy. "Imagine keeping *that* a secret!"

"Mom is out on a call," Mandy said as politely as she could. "And Dad is in the clinic."

"Then I'll just pop in to see him," Mrs. Ponsonby said, sweeping past her. "I can tell him about the new diet I've put darling Pandora on. *So* many vitamins. No wonder she's bouncing with health." She scooped up Pandora and called to Toby.

Mandy ground her teeth as Mrs. Ponsonby disappeared from view. She walked out into the backyard and closed the gate Mrs. Ponsonby had left wide open.

"Honestly, that woman thinks she can go anywhere, do anything," she said.

James looked resigned. "She usually can, that's the trouble," he said. "Nobody ever stands up to her."

Mandy began to walk softly across the grass, calling

to Shona. The little tan pony came to her at once, sniffling at her fingers. Mandy rubbed Shona's nose.

"Mrs. Ponsonby gave you a scare, didn't she, girl?" she said.

"She gave Polly an even bigger scare," said James. "And just as she was beginning to make friends with Shona."

Mandy nodded. "I'd better go and see how she is," she said. She looked at the Shetland pony.

"Shona's all right now," said James. "She was just startled." He hesitated. "Do you want me to come with you to see Polly?"

Mandy shook her head. "I don't think so, James," she said. She looked at Blackie, still standing patiently beside Shona. "But maybe Blackie could help."

Blackie wagged his tail at the sound of his name and Mandy gave him a pat on the head.

"You know, I think you're right about Blackie," James said. "He makes a good go-between for Polly and Shona."

Mandy smiled. "Thanks, James. I *hope* I'm right," she said. "And I hope Mrs. Ponsonby hasn't ruined everything!"

Mandy found Polly perched on the window seat in her bedroom.

"I've brought Blackie to see you," Mandy said.

Polly reached down as Blackie trotted into the room and went to her side.

"Has that big woman gone?" the little girl said, putting her arms around Blackie's neck.

Mandy sat down beside her. "It was only Mrs. Ponsonby," she said. "Mrs. Ponsonby is always like that."

Polly shook her head. "I'm not going to be a show jumper," she said. "I hate horses. They hurt people. Like . . . like . . ." Polly's lower lip began to tremble.

Mandy put an arm around Polly's shoulder. "Like your mom?" she said gently.

Polly nodded wordlessly, and two big tears rolled down her cheeks.

Mandy bit her lip. "That was a terrible accident," she said slowly. "But accidents *are* terrible." She drew a deep breath. "My real mom and dad were killed in a car accident when I was a baby," she went on. "But I don't hate cars. Your mom's horse couldn't help having a heart attack. It wasn't his fault."

Polly looked up at Mandy, her eyes swimming with tears. "But you've got a mom and dad," she said.

Mandy smiled. "The best in the world," she said. "They adopted me when I was a baby."

Polly buried her face in Blackie's neck and the

Labrador nestled closer to her. Mandy gave Polly time to think.

"Mommy started to teach me to ride," the little girl said at last. "She loved horses — like Daddy. Daddy would like me to ride Shona."

"I know Shona gave you a fright when her tail caught you across the cheek," Mandy said softly.

Polly looked up. "It wasn't Shona's fault," she said, then she bit her lip and buried her face in Blackie's neck again. "I mean, that woman scared her," she mumbled.

Mandy didn't dare to say anything else in case she said the wrong thing. Finally, Polly lifted her head and looked at Mandy.

"Is Shona all right?" she asked.

Mandy nodded. It was the first time Polly had called Shona by name. "She's fine," she said. "Why don't you come down and see?"

For a moment she thought Polly was going to refuse. Then the little girl slid off the window seat, still keeping a hand in the fur at Blackie's neck.

"Okay," she said. "If Blackie can come, too."

"Of course he can," Mandy said.

When Mandy and Polly came out into the backyard James could hardly believe his eyes. Polly went straight up to the little pony. She was still holding on tightly to Blackie but she put her free hand on Shona's neck.

"There," she said. "That horrible woman frightened me, too."

Shona whinnied softly and rubbed her head against Polly's neck. Polly laughed. "That tickles," she said.

Then Polly turned toward Mandy and James. "Do you think Susan would teach me to ride?" she said.

Mandy was speechless. She could only nod. After Mrs. Ponsonby's interference she had thought it would take weeks to get Polly anywhere near Shona again. Instead, it had put Polly on Shona's side against Mrs. Ponsonby. *Good old Mrs. Ponsonby*, Mandy thought. She had done them all a favor after all.

"I'm sure Susan will teach you to ride," James said to Polly. "You try and stop her!" He looked at Mandy. "And we'll be there, one on either side of you. Won't we, Mandy?"

Mandy nodded again. Then she got her voice back. "Oh, we will," she said fervently. "We certainly will!"

Six

"Terrific!" said Susan when Mandy called her. "I can't believe it. I'll come around tomorrow and we can start the lessons. I'd love to teach Polly to ride."

"We could come to the Beeches," Mandy said. But Susan didn't think that was a good idea.

"Not yet," she said. "Shona is used to Animal Ark. And we'll only be walking around on the first day. It's better that everything is as familiar as possible."

Mandy agreed. "Tomorrow, then," she said.

"You bet!" said Susan.

Mandy and Polly were up early the next morning.

Polly looked a little nervous but Dr. Adam and Dr. Emily were encouraging.

"I'll just come out and check on Shona," Dr. Adam said.

Mandy looked at her father gratefully. She knew Shona didn't really need checking over but Polly would feel better if Dr. Adam was there.

James arrived with Blackie just after breakfast and Polly looked a lot happier.

"Hello, Blackie," she said, getting down from the table. "Come and see Shona."

They all trooped out into the backyard and Dr. Adam unlatched the bottom half of the shed door and led Shona out.

"Let's have a look at you, Shona," he said.

Mandy watched as her father ran his capable hands over the Shetland pony's flanks and legs.

"She's certainly a fine, sturdy pony," he said to Polly. "Look how steady she is while I'm handling her."

Polly moved toward Shona. Blackie kept close to the little girl's heels. He seemed to know she needed him. Polly put out a hand and rubbed the pony's nose.

"She *is* gentle, isn't she?" Polly asked Dr. Adam.

Dr. Adam nodded. "The gentlest pony I've ever seen," he said. "Let's get her fed and watered."

"I'll get a bucket of water," Mandy said, heading for the kitchen.

When she came back, Polly was feeding handfuls of hay to Shona and the pony seemed to be enjoying it. Mandy put the bucket down in front of her and Shona dipped her head into it and began to drink. Then she threw up her head and shook it.

"Ow!" said Polly as a few drops of water landed on her. "I've already had my shower this morning, Shona." She laughed.

Mandy laughed, too. It looked as if things were going to work out just fine.

"We'd better muck out the shed now," James said. "We didn't give it a full cleaning yesterday."

Dr. Adam looked at his watch. "And I'd better start my rounds." He smiled. "See you later, everyone."

Mandy, James, and Polly began the mucking out. It was hard work. First Mandy raked out the old straw and James forked it into the wheelbarrow. Polly fetched the fresh new bedding while Mandy swept the shed floor. Finally, Polly spread the new straw evenly over the floor of the shed with a rake.

"Keeping a pony is hard work," James said, pushing his glasses up on his nose.

Mandy nodded. "Susan gets up really early every

morning to look after Prince," she said, wiping her forehead.

James looked at the fresh clean straw. "But it's worth it," he said. Then he grinned. "Still, I'm glad Blackie isn't this hard to look after!"

Blackie heard his name and came trotting up. James shut the shed door quickly. He didn't want Blackie tracking straw all over the yard. Blackie pawed at the shed door for a moment, then he gave up. He lolloped off down the yard, and soon he was busy chasing butterflies.

"He actually thinks he can catch them," James said, laughing as Blackie scampered after a huge Cabbage White. The butterfly promptly fluttered over the fence and out of reach, a shimmering patch of white against the blue of the sky.

Blackie watched it for a moment, then lay down on the grass and went to sleep in the sun. Mandy felt like doing the same after all their hard work. The spring sunshine was really hot now and the air full of the smell of fresh straw. She could hear birds chirping in the hedges under the garden fence. Blackie began to snore gently and Shona was nibbling delicately at the grass, making soft tearing noises. Mandy's eyes began to droop. But James had other ideas.

"Where's the saddle?" he asked. "We'd better have everything ready when Susan gets here."

"It's hanging on the back porch with the other tack," Mandy said, giving herself a shake. "I'll get it."

Soon they had the saddle and bridle, the bit and the reins out on the grass and were polishing and shining them to a high gloss. Polly knew exactly what to do.

"I've watched Daddy doing this lots of times," she said.

"Do you know where it all goes?" asked James, holding up a long strap and looking puzzled.

"That's the girth," said Polly. "It goes around the pony's middle to hold the saddle on."

"Oh, right," said James. "So what's this, then?" He held up another length of strap.

Polly giggled. "Silly," she said. "That's a stirrup leather."

"All these pieces look the same to me," said James.

Polly nodded. "But wait till we put them all together," she said. "Then you'll see what they're all for."

Mandy smiled. Polly was totally caught up in what she was doing. James was right. Looking after horses did seem to be in her blood.

"Doesn't it look lovely?" Mandy said when they had finished.

Polly looked up and rubbed her hand across her nose, leaving a streak of leather polish. "It smells lovely, too," she said.

Then a bicycle turned into the driveway. It was Susan.

"Ready for the lesson?" she said as she propped her bike against the side of the house.

Polly bit her lip and nodded. Mandy could see she was still a little nervous.

"Good," said Susan, pushing open the gate. "Let's get Shona saddled up."

Polly and Susan got to work, assembling the tack, showing Mandy and James what went where. Even Mandy was amazed when she saw all the different pieces of tack put together. Saddle and girth, stirrup leathers attached to the stirrups, and the even more complicated-looking bridle.

Susan looked at Polly. "Would you like me to put the bridle on the first time?" she asked.

Polly nodded. Mandy could see she was still wary of getting really close to Shona.

Susan picked up the bridle and reins and stood up, calling to Shona in a soft voice. She hitched the bridle over her shoulder and took a carrot out of her pocket. Then she stretched out her arm, holding the carrot flat on the palm of her hand. The Shetland pony came to her at once, sniffed at the carrot, and then began to nibble very gently at it.

Susan put her free arm round Shona's head, running her hands over the little pony's back, feeling her flanks. Then she leaned her weight on Shona's back. Shona stood solid as a rock.

"How long is it since she ate?" Susan asked.

"Mandy and I fed her about eight-thirty," Polly said.

Susan nodded. "She should be fine, then," she said. "You shouldn't ride a pony just after it's eaten."

Then Susan unhitched the bridle from her shoulder, still with her other hand on Shona's head. Standing with her back to Shona's tail, she slipped the reins over the pony's head and rested them just behind her ears. She brought her left hand under the bit and pressed it very gently against Shona's lips.

"If she doesn't open her mouth for the bit, a good trick is to put your thumb in the corner of her mouth and tickle her tongue," Susan said. "Most ponies can't help opening their mouths then."

But Shona opened her mouth beautifully to the bit and Susan slid the headpiece into place, bringing Shona's ears under it and smoothing out the hair underneath.

"She really is a gentle little thing," Susan said as she buckled up and adjusted the bridle. She looked at Polly. "Ready to help me saddle her up?"

This time Polly nodded eagerly. Mandy could see she was really interested in what Susan was doing. Polly heaved the saddle off the grass and walked toward Susan.

"I just hope Polly doesn't notice how good Susan is at taking care of ponies all of a sudden," James said.

"She thinks Susan is a very quick learner," Mandy said. Then she grinned. "Look at her. I'm sure she isn't thinking about anything but Shona at the moment!"

Mandy and James watched as Susan and Polly saddled Shona up, checking the girth, adjusting the stirrups, coming back again and again to the girth and tightening it a notch at a time.

"Ponies hate being girthed up tightly right away," Polly said, intent on her work.

Susan looked at Mandy and James over Polly's head and made a face. "She's terrific at this," she mouthed.

Mandy crossed her fingers and hoped that the riding lesson would go as well as this had.

Susan smiled down at Polly. "Okay," she said. "Where's your riding hat? You do have a hat, don't you?"

Polly nodded. "Daddy bought one for me when he bought the saddle and stuff. It's in my bedroom."

"You go and get it and I'll walk Shona around the garden to get her used to the saddle," Susan said.

Polly rushed off to get the riding hat, and Mandy looked at Susan.

"Do you think she'll be okay?" Susan asked.

"I've got all my fingers crossed," Mandy said. "She certainly isn't nearly as scared of Shona as she was."

Susan frowned. "If a rider is nervous, the pony feels it," she said.

James gave Shona a pat. "Shona will be all right with her, won't she, Blackie?"

Blackie gave a short bark as Polly ran back into the garden, fastening her riding hat under her chin.

"I'm ready," she said.

Mandy looked at her. She was a little pale, but her eyes were bright with eagerness.

"Okay," said Susan, leading Shona to stand beside her. "Mandy, can you hold Shona's head?"

Mandy held the pony still while Susan helped Polly to mount. As soon as the little pony felt someone on her back, she lifted her head and whinnied softly.

"It's okay, girl," said Mandy. "It's only Polly."

"All right?" Susan said to Polly.

Polly nodded. "All right," she repeated firmly.

Mandy looked up at Polly perched on Shona's back. It was clear that the little girl was trying hard not to be nervous. Susan was close by her side and James came to the other side. Blackie came behind as they set off around the yard.

Mandy laughed. "It's like a procession," she said.

"Or an honor guard," James said.

Polly didn't say anything. Her hands were gripping the reins rather tightly and her face was stiff with concentration.

"Try to relax your hands a little," Susan said. "And grip with your knees. How does the saddle feel? Comfy?"

Polly nodded and her hands relaxed just a little.

Susan kept talking to her, reassuring her, giving her instructions.

"Sit down into the saddle," Susan said. "But try to keep your back straight."

Mandy watched as Polly followed Susan's instructions.

"Like this?" she asked.

"Great!" said Susan. "You've got a very good seat, Polly. Do you know what that means?"

Polly giggled. "Everybody knows that," she said. "It's the way you sit on a horse."

Susan laughed. "Not *everybody* knows as much about horses as you do, Polly," she said. "You're a very smart girl."

Polly blushed with pleasure. Gradually, the tense look vanished from her face altogether and she began to look as if she was enjoying herself.

*   *   *

By the time the lesson was over, Polly was bubbling with excitement.

"Will you come tomorrow, Susan?" she asked.

Susan nodded. "I'll come every day," she said. "You're going to be a terrific rider, Polly. You're a natural. Just wait and see. By the end of the week, you'll be giving *me* lessons!"

Polly blushed again and looked pleased.

"I won't tell Daddy yet," she said. "I want it to be a surprise. It's his birthday soon. He'll be so pleased when he sees me riding Shona. And I'm going to get better every day."

Susan looked thoughtful. "How would you like to be my squire?" she said to Polly.

Polly looked puzzled. "What's that?" she asked.

"Well," said Susan. "I'm going to be a knight at the pageant, and every knight should have a squire. A squire is kind of like a groom. You could be mine."

"What would I have to do?" asked Polly.

Susan smiled. "You would ride beside me and Prince in the parade," she said.

"On Shona?" Polly said.

Susan nodded.

"In a parade?" Polly asked.

Susan nodded again. Polly's face lit up.

"You mean Daddy can come and see me riding in a parade?" she said. "Will Daddy be out of the hospital by then?"

Susan kept on nodding.

"Oh, wow!" said Polly. "I'd like that. I'd love to be your — what is it?"

"Squire," said Susan.

"Squire," repeated Polly. She looked overjoyed.

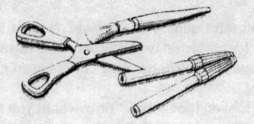

Seven

Polly *did* get better every day. Susan soon had the little girl and her pony out of the yard. Polly and Shona became a familiar sight in the village, Polly riding and Susan leading Shona down the main street to the bridle path that ran along the riverbank. Once Polly was really confident, Susan brought Prince along and the two ponies ambled side by side on their daily walks.

The bridle path was Polly's favorite trail.

"We went all the way down to the bridge today," she said at supper on Wednesday evening.

"The wooden bridge?" said Dr. Emily. "That's quite a distance."

Polly nodded. "You can see the hospital from there," she said. Her face lit up. "Maybe Susan and I could ride over to see Daddy one day."

Dr. Emily raised her eyebrows. "And what would the head nurse say about that?" she said. "I know she doesn't mind pets coming to visit the patients, but a pony!"

Polly giggled. "Imagine Daddy's face if I rode Shona right through the ward!" she said.

"The head nurse would have a fit," said Mandy. She smiled happily at Polly.

Polly was a changed girl. She was up early every morning to feed and water Shona and muck her out, and Mandy had loaned her every book about horses the Hopes possessed. Still it wasn't enough. Dr. Emily made several visits to the library in Walton with her.

Next to visiting her dad, riding Shona was Polly's favorite thing.

Polly looked out the window. "I can't wait for tomorrow," she said. "I wish I could ride Shona every minute of the day."

Dr. Adam laughed. "I don't know if Shona would be too happy about that," he said.

Outside Mandy noticed that clouds were rolling down the fields. The hot spell was coming to an end. A spatter of sudden rain splashed against the windowpanes.

"Uh-oh," said Dr. Adam. "That looks as if it's settling in for the night."

"Shona!" said Polly, jumping down from the table. "I'd better put her in the shed before she gets wet."

Dr. Adam shook his head as the little girl scampered out the door. "She'd have that pony sleeping at the end of her bed if she could," he said. Then he looked at Mandy. "Well done, Mandy," he said. "She really seems to have overcome her distrust of horses."

Mandy blushed. "It's Susan who's done the most," she said. "She's been terrific with Polly."

"Yes, but it was your suggestion in the first place," Dr. Adam pointed out.

Dr. Emily looked out at the rain. "It's getting heavier," she said. "I hope it doesn't last for days. That field down by the church gets so waterlogged."

The field by the church was where the pageant was to take place. The parade would start at the far end of the village and proceed all the way through Welford until it reached the church. Then all the events would be held in Farmer Redpath's field.

"The pageant!" Mandy said. She giggled. "I can just imagine Mrs. Ponsonby squishing about in her long dress and her boots."

"Don't forget about the rest of us," said her mom.

"The rain won't last that long," Mandy said. "The pageant isn't until Saturday. It's only Wednesday." She looked at her mom. "Will Mr. Hurst be able to come?" she asked.

Dr. Emily smiled. "I told the head nurse about Polly being Susan's squire," she said. "She thinks Mr. Hurst should be just about ready to leave by Saturday. Just in time for Polly's surprise. He's out of traction now."

"Oh, good," said Mandy. "It would be a real shame if he missed seeing Polly." Then she got up. "I'd better go and give her a hand with Shona."

Polly had Shona tucked up snugly in the shed with a blanket over her. Rain drummed on the roof of the shed but inside it was cozy and warm.

"You don't think she'll catch cold, do you?" Polly said.

Mandy smiled. "The shed is watertight," she said. "Shona will be fine. Her coat is very thick and shaggy. Don't you worry."

Polly gave the little pony a pat. "And now I'm going to make Daddy a birthday card," she said. "It's his birthday on Friday."

"And Mom says he'll be out of the hospital on Saturday — in time to see you in the pageant," Mandy said.

Polly smiled. "I know," she said. "He's got that horrible pulley thing off now, and the head nurse is going to give him a pair of crutches." She laughed. "I think I'll put a rabbit on his birthday card."

"Why a rabbit?" Mandy said as they closed the shed door and made a dash for the house.

"Because rabbits hop," said Polly. "And Daddy will have to hop for a while."

Mandy smiled. Everything was working out for Polly. She loved Shona, and her dad was getting better. Mandy looked back out at the rain as she shook the water droplets from her hair. It was bouncing off the path now, coming down in great, heavy sheets. She could hardly see the shed at the bottom of the garden. Rain that heavy couldn't last long.

But the rain did last. The next day it rained all day and by Friday, Mandy thought it would never stop.

She and James were sitting at the kitchen table in Animal Ark when the phone rang. They were making the pennants for the pageant. The table was covered with colored paper. They were cutting out triangles of paper and sticking them onto long bamboo poles. Meanwhile Polly was finishing her birthday card, her tongue poking out of the side of her mouth in concentration.

"*How* many of these do we have to make?" asked James.

Mandy made a face. "We should have started sooner," she said.

"I'll help you," Polly said. "I've nearly finished my card."

"Thanks, Polly," Mandy said. "Mrs. Ponsonby will have a fit if we don't finish them in time."

"You're right there," said Dr. Emily, coming into the kitchen. "She said she was going to come over this afternoon and get them."

Mandy looked at the pile of paper and the bundle of bamboo sticks.

"Yikes," said James. "We'll have to get a move on."

Mandy looked at her mother. She looked worried about something. "What's wrong, Mom?" she asked.

"There's an emergency at Twyford Farm," Dr. Emily said. "I'll have to get up there."

"What kind of emergency?" Mandy asked with concern.

"One of Mr. Hapwell's prize herd slipped in the mud coming into the barn," Dr. Emily said. "She's only a young calf but she can't get up. It looks as if her leg might be broken."

"Oh, poor thing. Can I come?" Mandy said.

Dr. Emily shook her head. "You stay here and look after Polly," she replied. "And besides, you've got those pennants to finish. I might be a while."

"Will you be back for evening office hours?" Mandy asked.

Dr. Emily nodded. "It's just a pity your dad had to go to that meeting in York today," she said. "I could have used the Land Rover but he's taken it. I didn't think I'd need it. I'll have to go in the car."

Mandy frowned. Twyford Farm was high up on a hill.

"Be careful on the road," Mandy said.

Her mother smiled. "I've driven that road a thousand times," she said. "Don't you worry."

But Mandy looked out at the rain still pouring down. The roads would be bad — especially the dirt farm tracks.

"I'll be back in time to take you over to the hospital before evening office hours, Polly," Dr. Emily said to the little girl.

"Will the calf need to have her leg put in traction like Daddy?" Polly asked.

Dr. Emily smiled. "I shouldn't think so," she said. "That *would* give me a bit of a problem!"

Polly held up her card. "Do you think Daddy will like it?" she said.

Dr. Emily looked at the bright pink rabbit. "I think he'll love it," she said. "See you later. Jean and Simon will deal with any calls while I'm away."

Mandy nodded as her mother shrugged on a raincoat and went out by the back door. She listened to the car driving away. Mandy hoped Mr. Hapwell's calf would be all right.

James brushed glue onto the edge of a paper triangle and wrapped it around a bamboo pole. "Come on, Mandy," he said.

Mandy picked up another pole. "You know, these will look really good at the parade," she said.

"Can I have one to carry?" Polly asked.

Mandy nodded. "Everybody in the parade will have one. Then when we get to the field, we'll stick them in the ground all around the edge. It'll look terrific."

"*If* we get them finished," James said. "And if it ever stops raining!"

Mandy and James worked steadily until they heard the sound of a car in the driveway.

"Mom can't be back yet," said Mandy.

James went to the window and peered out through the rain. "Oh, no! It's Mrs. Ponsonby," he said. Then he grinned as he looked at Mandy's face. "She looks like a giant melon."

The back door banged and Mrs. Ponsonby sailed into the kitchen. She was wearing an enormous bright yellow plastic raincoat and a matching rain hat. For final insurance against the weather she was carrying a yellow umbrella. She flapped her umbrella, scattering drops of water all over the room. She had a big plastic bag over one arm.

"I don't have much time," she said as she plumped herself down at the table. "I've left darling Toby and Pandora at home. I didn't want to bring them out in all this nasty rain. So I *must* get back."

"Hello, Mrs. Ponsonby," Mandy said.

Polly shrank in her chair. She didn't like Mrs. Ponsonby much. Not since she had frightened Shona.

Mrs. Ponsonby charged straight on. "Haven't you finished those pennants yet?" she said. "We need them for tomorrow, you know."

"We've *nearly* finished," said James. "There were quite a few. It's a lot of hard work."

"Hmmph!" said Mrs. Ponsonby. "Young people today don't know the meaning of hard work. I'll take the ones you've finished and pick up the rest later on this evening."

"Aye-aye, Mrs. Ponsonby," Mandy said under her breath.

"What was that, Mandy dear?" Mrs. Ponsonby said.

"Nothing," Mandy said.

But Mrs. Ponsonby wasn't listening. She reached into the plastic bag and brought out a funny-shaped object.

"Now," she said. "Where's your mother, Mandy? I want some advice about my hennin."

Mandy looked at the object sitting on the table. It looked like two upturned cones stuck onto a bowl-shaped thing. There were wires sticking out of it.

"Your what?" she said.

Mrs. Ponsonby scrabbled in the bag again and took out what looked like a net curtain.

"My hennin," she said, pointing to the object. "It's a sort of hat. The sort that ladies wore in medieval times."

"Oh," said Mandy. "Mom's isn't like that. It's a tall, pointy hat."

"They came in different shapes," Mrs. Ponsonby said. "This, Mandy dear, is a butterfly hennin."

"What are those wires for?" said James.

Mrs. Ponsonby draped the net curtain over the wires and held the hennin up. "It's supposed to look like butterfly wings," she said.

Mandy looked at the twisted bits of wire. It didn't look anything like a butterfly. In fact it looked to Mandy more like a television antenna!

"Mom had to go out on an emergency call," she said.

"Oh, that's too bad," said Mrs. Ponsonby. "Still, I'll take the pennants and leave the hennin with you. I'm sure your mother can fix it."

Mandy nodded. She had learned long ago that the

only thing to do when Mrs. Ponsonby was around was
to agree.

Mrs. Ponsonby gathered up the completed pennants
and looked down at Polly's card. "What a nice doggie,
dear," she said.

Polly looked at the rabbit and her bottom lip trem-
bled. "It's a rabbit," she said.

"Mrs. Ponsonby's glasses are a bit steamed up from

the rain," Mandy said quickly, giving Mrs. Ponsonby a look. "Aren't they, Mrs. Ponsonby?"

Mrs. Ponsonby blinked at Mandy and looked at Polly's trembling lip. Then she nodded. "Of course they are," she said kindly to Polly. "I see it now. Silly me! It's a lovely rabbit, dear. Maybe I need new glasses."

Mandy shook her head. That was the trouble with Mrs. Ponsonby. Most of the time she was absolutely awful, but sometimes she could be quite nice. She really didn't *mean* to hurt people.

"I'll tell Mom about the hat," Mandy said.

"*Hennin,* dear," said Mrs. Ponsonby as she picked up her umbrella and made for the door. "And tell your father I want a last-minute word with him about the booths at the pageant. If only this rain would stop! We've got such a lot of money to raise. Honestly, that church roof simply swallows money."

Mandy had a vision of the church roof opening up and gulping down sacks of cash.

James looked at the hennin as Mrs. Ponsonby slammed the back door behind her. "People didn't really wear those things, did they?" he said.

Mandy nodded. "Five hundred years ago they did," she said. "But something tells me they didn't look much like that one."

"Those look like horns," Polly said, pointing to the

cones. "I don't think Mrs. Ponsonby is very smart. She couldn't tell the difference between a dog and a rabbit!" Polly sounded outraged.

Mandy smiled. "Your dad will know the difference," she said.

Polly's face lit up. "I'm really looking forward to seeing him," she said. "I haven't missed a *single* day."

The telephone rang and Mandy rose to answer it. It was her mother. She sounded out of breath.

"Are you all right, Mom?" Mandy said.

"I'm fine," Dr. Emily replied.

"And how is Mr. Hapwell's calf?" Mandy said.

"She's fine, too," Dr. Emily said. "It was only a green-stick fracture. The bone was partly broken, partly bent. But I've put a cast on it and sedated her. She'll be as right as rain in no time at all."

"Don't talk about rain," Mandy said jokingly.

"I'm afraid I won't be back for a while," Dr. Emily said. "The car broke down halfway along the farm track on my way up. Once I'm finished here, I'll have to wait until someone can come out and take a look at it. But at least the rain has stopped now. Thank goodness. The river looked as if it was about to burst its banks when I passed it earlier on."

"Poor Mom," said Mandy.

"Poor Polly," said Dr. Emily. "I won't have time to take her to the hospital after all. I'll only just get home in time for evening office hours. Will you tell her?"

"Of course," said Mandy. "I'm sure she'll understand."

But when Mandy went through to the kitchen and told Polly, her face fell.

"But it's Daddy's birthday today," she said. "I've made him a card."

"I'm sorry, Polly," Mandy said. "You can phone him. That would be nearly as good. They've got cell phones at the hospital. The nurse will bring one right to your dad's bed."

But Polly refused to be cheered up. "I think I'll go out and see Shona," she said finally, still sulking.

Mandy smiled. That sounded like a good idea. If anything could cheer Polly up, it would be Shona. "The rain has stopped at last," she said. "Maybe you could let her out for a walk in the yard."

Polly nodded but she didn't look very happy as she went out.

"Poor kid," said James. "She's really upset."

"It had to be the day Dad was away as well," Mandy said.

"Perhaps we could take her," said James. "She could ride on the back of my bike."

"Mom wouldn't like that," said Mandy. "It's too dangerous and besides, we've still got these pennants to finish."

James nodded. "I suppose you're right," he said, picking up another pole. "We'd better get on with it, then."

Mandy settled down to work. There seemed to be an awful lot of pennants still to do.

The next time the phone rang, Mandy rushed to answer it. "Maybe Mom hasn't managed to get the car fixed yet," she said.

But it was Mrs. Ponsonby.

"Mandy Hope," Mrs. Ponsonby said into the telephone. "I don't know what's gotten into you — letting that little girl ride by herself in this weather!"

"What?" said Mandy. "Do you mean Polly?"

"Of course I mean Polly," said Mrs. Ponsonby. "I've just seen her in the village."

"But you couldn't have," said Mandy. "Polly is here, Mrs. Ponsonby."

"Then who did I see riding down High Street five minutes ago?" Mrs. Ponsonby said.

Mandy frowned. "It couldn't have been Polly," she said.

"Are you quite sure about that?" Mrs. Ponsonby said. "It certainly looked like Polly."

"I'm absolutely sure," Mandy said.

"Then I must have been mistaken," said Mrs. Ponsonby. "It must have been somebody else but I can't think who. Maybe I really do need new glasses. It certainly isn't like me to make a mistake."

And with that, she hung up.

"What was that all about?" James said, looking at Mandy's puzzled face.

Mandy shook her head. "I don't understand," she said. "Mrs. Ponsonby says she saw Polly riding Shona down High Street."

"When?" said James.

"About five minutes ago," Mandy said. "But Polly has been here all afternoon."

"When did Polly go out to see Shona?" James asked.

Mandy looked at him. "I don't know, half an hour ago maybe. We were so busy with these pennants I didn't notice the time." She stopped. "You don't think she's taken Shona out on her own, do you? She wouldn't do that."

"We'd better check that she's still here," James said. "Just to be on the safe side."

Mandy was out of the door before him, running toward the shed at the bottom of the garden. The shed door was wide open. There was no sign of Polly or Shona.

"The saddle and bridle are missing, too," James said, running after her.

Mandy looked at him. "She's gone," she said. "She's taken Shona and she's gone — but why?"

"Never mind that now," said James. "We'd better go after her. Where on earth do you think she was going?"

Mandy bit her lip. "Where she always goes, I suppose," she said. "The bridle path."

"We'll take our bikes," James said, heading for the gate.

Mandy thought of something else. "Oh, no," she said. "The bridle path runs along the riverbank. Mom said the river looked as if it might burst its banks. James, Polly could be in real danger!"

Eight

Mandy and James leaped for their bikes.

"The hospital!" Mandy yelled at James. "I'll bet that's where she's going. It's her dad's birthday, remember?"

"She must be planning on crossing the river by the wooden bridge," James yelled back as they mounted the bikes and pushed off.

"That bridle path will be really slippery," Mandy said as they set off. "It won't be safe."

The mud spattered up from their wheels as they raced down the road from Animal Ark to the village. There was nobody around, even though the rain had stopped now. Hedges and trees still dripped water but a pale sun was trying to struggle through.

They pedaled down High Street toward the trail that led to the bridle path and then they were off the road, wheels churning on the muddy ground.

Mandy's tires spun as they tried to grip the surface; she pushed the bike on, willing it to grip, forcing it to hold to the trail.

James skidded sideways, then curved around a huge puddle. Mandy went straight through it, the water whooshing up in a great fountain around her, soaking her. But she didn't care. All she wanted to do was to find Polly.

The bike journey seemed very slow. The mud sucked at the wheels, holding them back, slowing them down. But at last they were off the trail and onto the bridle path.

Mandy's heart turned over as she looked at the river. It had risen almost to the top of the bank, rushing and roaring in a great muddy torrent as it swept branches and leaves in its path. Her bike skidded and she jammed on the brakes, plowing into the mud. She stopped just short of the bank.

Mandy looked down into the water swirling below her. What if Shona had slipped on the muddy path? What if Polly had fallen off? She wasn't an experienced rider; she was only a little girl.

Mandy jerked her bike around and pushed off again. James was ahead now, rounding a bend in the bridle path. Mandy heard him yell and saw him glance around quickly at her. Then he had rounded the bend and was out of sight.

Mandy pedaled as hard as she could. Her legs felt as if they were on fire and the bike was heavy with all the mud clinging to its wheels. Then she rounded the bend, too, and almost crashed into James. His bike was firmly stuck in the mud.

"You go on," he shouted to her. "My bike won't make it. The mud is too deep."

Mandy tried to push off but it was no good. There was too much mud for her bike, too. The wheels sank into the thick brown ooze. She looked up. James was getting off his bike, throwing it down at the side of the path.

Mandy did the same and together they began to run along the bridle path.

"There she is!" James yelled suddenly. He pointed into the distance. Mandy looked ahead. A small figure on a pony was just approaching the wooden bridge that crossed the racing river.

"Polly!" Mandy yelled.

But they were too far away to be heard. They ran on, legs pumping, breath coming in short gasps.

Polly and Shona got to the bridge. Mandy could see that they were going to cross it. Shona stepped forward onto the bridge, then stopped short. Polly bent over the Shetland pony's neck and tapped with her heels. Still Shona didn't move.

"Polly!" Mandy yelled again. "Wait for us!"

But Polly didn't turn around. Shona was backing off the bridge onto the bridle path. Polly tried to force her forward but the little pony shied and kept backing away.

Mandy was running so fast, she began to get a stitch in her side. Then James yelled again. "Look!" he shouted at Mandy. "She's getting down."

"Thank goodness," Mandy panted. "She must have heard me."

But Polly hadn't. Mandy saw her dismount and take hold of Shona's reins. Then she tried to lead the stubborn pony over the bridge. Shona stood rock-solid, unmoving. Polly pulled on the reins but still Shona didn't move. Polly tugged harder, trying to drag Shona onto the bridge but Shona pulled back, pulling Polly away from the bridge.

Mandy watched the scene as she ran. She was too out of breath to yell now and the stitch in her side was getting worse. It was as if Polly and Shona were having a tug-of-war.

Then an incredible thing happened. Polly came back to Shona's side, patting the little pony's flanks, urging her forward. But Shona turned on Polly and nudged her. Polly's feet slipped in the mud and she almost fell under

Shona. She tried to scramble up but Shona pushed her back onto the ground, holding her there with her head firmly on Polly's chest.

Mandy and James were nearly there now. Mandy put on a final burst of speed as the little girl began to scream.

Oh, no, she thought as the hysterical sobs shattered the air. All their good work had gone for nothing. Polly would never recover from a fright like this.

Shona stood there unmoving with Polly pinned to the ground. Behind them, the river roared on its way downstream, the sound mingling with Polly's screams.

Mandy reached them just before James.

"It's all right," she said, making a dive for Polly. "It's all right, Polly, we're here."

The little girl turned her tearstained face toward Mandy and tried to scramble to her feet. Mandy put out her hand to push Shona's head away from her but the pony lifted her head before Mandy could touch it and took a step back.

"Mandy!" cried Polly, throwing herself into Mandy's arms. "Take her away! Take her away! I hate horses. I told you! She tried to hurt me. I told you!"

"Hush," said Mandy. She cradled the little girl in her arms, soothing her as best she could. "You're okay now, Polly. You're quite safe."

James went to Shona and took her reins in his hands. Then he turned toward Mandy, his face concerned.

"What on earth happened?" he said. "What was Shona doing?"

Mandy looked at him over the little girl's head. "I don't know," she said. "I just don't understand it. Shona is so gentle."

"No, she isn't," Polly said with a sob. "She's horrible. She pushed me over. She wouldn't let me get up. She wouldn't even go across the bridge. And I wanted to see Daddy. I *promised* him I'd come every day and it's his *birthday*." She finished on another sob.

Mandy looked down at her. "Maybe Shona was frightened of the water," she said. "The river is really high. That bridge isn't very strong."

"But she pushed me over," Polly repeated.

Mandy looked beyond her at the river. It cascaded under the bridge, whirling against the supports. As she watched, a tree branch hurtled past, crashing into the middle support. Mandy heard the support creak with the impact. Her eyes opened wide and she let go of Polly.

"Stay here," she said. "Don't move." She walked toward the bridge.

"Where are you going?" said James.

Shona jerked the reins in his hand and pulled away

toward Mandy. Mandy looked around at the pony, then at the bridge again. Very carefully she put a hand on the wooden rail and a foot on the planking.

Shona dragged James forward, trying to get to Mandy. But Mandy wasn't going anywhere — not anymore! She had seen what Shona knew already. There was a big crack across one of the bridge supports — the middle one. It could collapse at any minute.

"It's all right, girl," she said, coming back to the pony. "It's all right. Good girl."

Polly turned furiously on her. "How can you say that?" she said. "She's bad. I hate her."

Mandy opened her mouth to speak, but before she could, James said, "Wow! Look at that!"

She turned. Another tree branch, a huge one this time, was hurtling down the river, churning up the water as it went. It had collected a lot of debris as it came downriver. There were other branches and sticks and cardboard boxes and bits of wood tangled in the branch. It reached the bridge and crashed into it, right where the middle support was. There was a tearing sound and a long, groaning creak. Then the bridge seemed to sway and, almost in slow motion, the middle section started to crumple.

Mandy and James watched in horror as the whole bridge sagged. The middle part gave way entirely. Timber and planks crashed into the river and went whirling away downstream on the current.

James stared at the sagging, broken bridge. "Yikes!" he said. "Polly, it really is lucky you didn't cross that bridge."

Mandy looked at the other two. "It wasn't luck," she said. "Shona knew the bridge was unsafe. She must have seen the crack in the support. She must have felt the whole thing give the moment she stepped onto the bridge. That's why she wouldn't go any farther. And that's why she knocked Polly over and kept her down. She was trying to stop Polly from walking onto the bridge."

James looked at Shona in amazement. "Wow!" he said. "What a pony!"

Mandy bent down and comforted the little girl. "Shona wasn't trying to hurt you, Polly," she said. "She was trying to protect you. She saved your life."

Polly looked up at Mandy, her eyes huge.

"Shona?" she said wonderingly. Then she looked past Mandy at the swirling river. "I would have fallen in there," she said. "I can't swim."

Mandy nodded. Polly turned to look at the Shetland pony. Shona was standing quietly beside them. Polly reached up and put her arms around the pony's neck.

"Oh, Shona," she said, rubbing her face against

Shona's mane, "you didn't want to hurt me. You saved me. You like me." Polly turned back to Mandy and James, her face lit up. "Isn't Shona just the most wonderful pony in the world?" she said.

At that moment the sun burst through the clouds, sparkling on the rushing river, coating the trees with gold, dancing among the droplets of water on Shona's shaggy mane.

James and Mandy looked at each other and Mandy had to swallow quite hard. Then she smiled back at Polly.

"Oh, she is," she said. "The very best!"

Nine

"Where on earth have you been?" Simon asked as Mandy, James, Polly, and Shona arrived at the door of Animal Ark. Then he looked up as car wheels sounded on gravel. "There's your mom," he said.

Dr. Emily got out of the car and looked at their mud-spattered clothes. "What happened?" she said at once. "Did Polly have a fall?"

Mandy gave her a reassuring smile. "Not exactly," she said. "It's okay now, Mom. Honestly, it is."

Dr. Emily looked at Polly's face. The little girl still looked a bit pale. Mandy could see her mom making up her mind to attend to Polly first.

"I don't know if I like the sound of that," she said. She

113

cast an expert eye over the Shetland pony. "Mandy, you and James give Shona a quick rubdown and stable her. I'll take Polly inside and get her cleaned up."

Mandy and James took Shona around and to the shed, rubbed her down, and gave her some food. By the time they arrived in the kitchen, Polly was sitting up at the big wooden table, drinking tea and eating muffins. Jean and Simon were there, too.

"Do you think Shona should get a medal the way people do?" the little girl was asking Dr. Emily. "She deserves a medal for saving my life."

"I'll say she does," Simon said. "But you know, you shouldn't have run off like that, Polly."

Polly bit her lip. "I know that now," she said. "I'm sorry."

Dr. Emily smiled but there was a tiny frown between her eyebrows. "Just as long as you never do anything like that again, Polly," she said. She looked around as Mandy and James came in. "And why didn't you two call for help? Jean and Simon were both here."

Mandy bit her lip and sat down beside her mother. "We didn't think," she said. "We were only thinking of catching up with Polly."

"And a good thing, too, if you ask me," Jean said. "Polly might have gotten away from Shona and tried to run across that bridge."

But Polly shook her head. "Oh, no," she said confidently. "Shona wouldn't have let me do that." Her eyes lit up and she grinned impishly. "Shona would have sat on me first," she said.

Everybody laughed — even Dr. Emily. Mandy watched with relief as the tiny frown faded from between her mother's eyes. She tucked her hand through Dr. Emily's arm.

"Sorry, Mom," she said.

Dr. Emily shook her head. "If I go gray overnight, you'll know why," she said. "Just don't go doing anything dramatic at the pageant tomorrow."

"Yikes," said James. "The pennants! Mrs. Ponsonby will skin us alive if we don't get them finished in time."

Mandy and James quickly set to work. They *did* get the pennants finished in time. But when Mrs. Ponsonby came to collect them, she was much more interested in Polly's story.

"I told you I saw her," she said to Mandy and James triumphantly.

Mandy looked at the large woman. "Of course you did," she said. "I've only just realized it. If you hadn't phoned then, we'd never have known Polly was missing. Mrs. Ponsonby, you're a hero!"

Mrs. Ponsonby blushed as pink as the roses on her hat. "Heroine, dear," she said. "Ladies are heroines."

"Just like Shona," Polly said with a smile.

*   *   *

On Saturday, the sun was shining through the windows of the residential unit where Mandy was finishing up cleaning the cages. She had already put on her costume for the pageant. She held a tiny kitten up and looked at it seriously.

"Now, I want you to be good while I'm at the pageant," she said to it. "And I promise I'll come and play with you as soon as I get back."

The kitten batted a paw at the feather in Mandy's green velvet cap, and Mandy laughed as the cap slid sideways.

"Not yet," she said. "You can have the feather to play with *after* the pageant."

"Are you coming, Mandy?" Dr. Adam asked from the doorway of the residential unit. "The pageant is due to start in ten minutes. You don't want to miss the parade, do you?"

Mandy put the kitten back in its cage and fastened the catch.

"Coming," she said, turning around.

Then she stopped. "Oh, Dad, you look fabulous!" she said.

Dr. Adam stood at the door, fingering his beard.

"I don't know about that," he said, looking down at

the long deep red robe he was wearing. "I feel like an idiot."

Mandy inspected his costume. It came almost to her father's feet and was trimmed with fur.

"*Fake* fur," Dr. Adam said, seeing the direction of Mandy's eyes.

"That's all right, then," said Mandy, grinning. "Where's Mom?"

Dr. Adam smiled. "Lady Emily?" he said. "She looks wonderful! Come on, we're all waiting for you."

Mandy slipped off the lab coat she was wearing over her costume. She smoothed down the tabard and gave her tights a tug. Then she plonked her page's cap more securely on her head, tickled the kitten under the chin, and followed her father out of the residential unit.

"Wow!" she said as she saw her mother. "You look amazing, Mom."

Dr. Emily was dressed in a grass-green gown, held at the waist by a heavy gold belt. Her bright red hair cascaded down her back from under her hennin. Mandy wrinkled her forehead as she looked at the tall, pointy hat with the veil trailing from it.

"How are you going to keep that on?" she said.

"Willpower," said Dr. Emily. "Let's just hope it isn't windy this afternoon." She looked at Mandy. "You

know, that tabard really suits you. I only see you in
jeans during vacations."

Mandy looked down. The tabard came down to her
knees. She was wearing a white T-shirt and a pair of
thick black tights under it. Her cap slipped a little and
she pushed it back up on her head.

"You should hear what James had to say about the
costumes," she said. "I gave him a pair of my school
tights to wear."

Dr. Emily laughed. "I don't think I want to hear what
James had to say about *that*," she said.

"Right," said Jean Knox, bustling in from Reception
and dragging Simon after her. "Everybody ready, then?"

"I feel ridiculous," Simon said, running a hand
through his fair hair. He was dressed as a knight with a
long white cape over cardboard chain mail. The cape
had a large red cross on it and Simon was carrying a
two-handed sword.

"You look great," said Mandy. "That sword looks
real."

"Jean made it," Simon said, grinning. "I'm her knight
in shining armor."

"Huh!" said Jean. "Let's hope I don't need to be rescued, then."

Jean was wearing a full-skirted robe in bright blue. It

had a hood that reached all the way down her back. The hood had gotten tangled up in Jean's glasses' chain.

Mandy untangled the hood for her. "Polly is out in the yard with Shona," she said.

"Let's get this show on the road, then," said Dr. Adam, leading the way.

Mandy followed him into the yard. "Polly, you look terrific!" she said as the little girl came riding up on Shona.

Polly was wearing dark brown riding breeches and a leather waistcoat over her white shirt.

The little girl flushed. "Shona looks lovely, too," she said.

Mandy looked at the little tan Shetland pony. Polly had been hard at work. She had braided Shona's thick mane and twined colored ribbons into it. There were more colored ribbons twisted around the reins and bridle.

"Shona looks great," said Mandy as they set off, Polly riding, the others walking. "All ready to surprise your father."

They made their way down the path from Animal Ark to the village. The sun was hot once again; it was as if it had never rained at all. Mandy felt a surge of happiness. The sun was shining, the sky was blue, birds twittered in the hedge, and Polly loved her pony. Life couldn't be more perfect!

"Yikes!" said Mandy as they reached High Street. "Look at everybody!"

"It looks as if somebody has turned the clock back five hundred years," said Dr. Emily. "Mrs. Ponsonby should be pleased. *Everybody* has dressed up."

High Street was a sea of color. There was red and blue and green bunting hanging from every storefront and strung between the lampposts. Mr. Hardy had draped a huge yellow flag with a red lion on it from an upstairs window of the Fox and Goose and everywhere Mandy looked, people were waving yellow and orange and purple pennants. The village was swarming with people in medieval costumes. And not just people! There were animals of all kinds. The sound of barking dogs mixed with children shouting. Farther up the street, horses whinnied as their riders assembled for the procession.

The Spry sisters from the Riddings were there. The elderly twins were dressed in multicolored veils and gowns with huge long trains, looking, as always, like doubles of each other. Miss Marjorie waved to Mandy, knocking Miss Joan's headdress off in her enthusiasm. Mandy waved back and Miss Marjorie tripped over her train.

"They'll be lucky if they make it as far as the field," Simon said, laughing. "Look, there's Lydia with Houdini."

Mandy looked across the crowd at a short-haired woman dressed in breeches and a brown woolen jerkin. It was Lydia Fawcett from High Cross Farm, and she was trying to stop a determined-looking, black-and-white goat from eating a dangling string of bunting.

"And I forgot to bring my camera," Simon said, shaking his head.

"There's Mr. Hardy," said Mandy, pointing to a youngish man in a leather jerkin.

"And look at Mr. and Mrs. McFarlane," said Jean as the couple came out of the general store.

Mrs. McFarlane waved and her husband brandished an ax at them.

"The woodcutter and his wife," Dr. Emily said. "Let's hope that ax is only cardboard."

Then a figure in shining armor rode up. Mandy gasped. Susan and Prince looked tremendous. Susan's helmet plumes and Prince's caparison were exactly the same shade of blue. Susan had trimmed the caparison in gold and silver and had wound red-and-white tape around her lance. She smiled down at them through the visor of her helmet.

"Wow!" said Simon.

"Hi, Sir Simon," said Susan, grinning at him. "Great sword!"

"You look terrific," Mandy said. "And so does Prince."

Susan smiled with pleasure. "Thanks, Mandy," she said.

There was a booming sound from farther down the street. It was Mrs. Ponsonby with a megaphone, trying to organize the crowd.

Susan looked at Polly. "Come on, Polly. We're at the head of the procession."

Mandy watched as Sir Susan and her squire rode off. Susan's armor was only silver cardboard but it glittered in the sun like the real thing, and the plumes in her helmet waved in the breeze. Polly, the perfect squire, rode proudly behind on Shona.

"I guess I'd better go and join the other knights," Simon said. "See you later."

Mandy gazed around her, amazed. She had never expected it to be as good as this. It really was as if she had stepped back in time.

"Now, now, come along there!" said a booming voice.

Mrs. Ponsonby was sailing down the street, her purple velvet gown billowing behind her. Someone must have taken her megaphone away but she seemed to be doing all right without it. There was an enormous red bow pinned to the bodice of her dress. Pandora was tucked under one arm and a bundle of pennants was under the other. Toby and Pandora were wearing matching bright pink coats with silver dragons on them. Toby was barking loudly around Mrs. Ponsonby's feet; she was in severe danger of tripping over him.

"Hello, Mrs. Ponsonby," Mandy said. "Have you seen James?"

Mrs. Ponsonby shook her head impatiently and her

hennin wobbled. "I've got enough to do without looking for James Hunter," she said. "Your grandpa and Walter Pickard have gone down to the church to start the bell-ringing. *Do* get into line, Mandy dear."

Mrs. Ponsonby's hennin was tilted at an angle and she gave it a prod with one of the pennants she was carrying, trying to straighten it.

"Here you are, one each," she said, handing out pennants right and left. "And make sure to *wave* them!"

Mandy looked around for James but neither he nor Blackie were anywhere to be seen. Then the church bells started pealing out and everyone got into line and started to walk down to the field by the church, waving their pennants obediently.

Mandy had to admit it: Mrs. Ponsonby had done a good job. The procession wound its way into the field with the riders in front, the sun flashing from banners and flags and pennants. The church bells rang out, mingling with the jingle of horse harnesses and the excited squeals of children. The field was ringed with booths and tents selling muffins and pancakes, toffee apples, and cotton candy. The tents were decorated with bunting and the trestle tables inside were loaded with goodies.

The booths were just as good. There was a ringtoss and a Jacob's ladder, a fortune-teller's booth decorated with suns and moons, a booth selling stained glass, and another with pottery displayed in gleaming ranks. There was even a target set up for archery.

"Oh, I'd love to try that," said Mandy, looking at the bull's-eye target as they passed it.

"Ernie has done a great job with that castle," Dr. Adam said.

Mandy turned around. Ernie Bell's castle was at the far end of the field. It looked marvelous with its painted turrets and its brightly colored flags blowing in the breeze.

Mandy sniffed. There were wonderful smells coming from some of the booths. "Mmm," she said to her mother. "I feel hungry already."

Dr. Emily laughed. "You've only just had lunch," she said.

"But food in the open air is so much better," Mandy replied. "And besides, Grandma promised to set up a doughnut stand."

"Did they have doughnuts in medieval times?" Dr. Adam said.

"Maybe," Dr. Emily replied. "But I don't think they had cotton candy!"

"There's James," Mandy said as they turned into the field.

She could just make out his green cap with the feather in it.

"Hi, James!" she yelled. "Over here."

James began to squirm through the crowd toward them. Mandy plunged her pennant into the ground and squeezed her way toward him.

"Where have you been?" she said as Blackie threw himself at her in welcome.

James grinned. "I had to chase Blackie three times around the yard," he said. "He ran off with a part of my costume."

Mandy looked James over from head to toe.

"Sweatpants!" she said. "What happened to the tights I gave you?"

James grinned even more. "That was the part Blackie ran away with," he said, looking down at his pet. "Isn't he awful? He tore a huge hole in them. I couldn't wear them like that. I'll have to buy you a new pair."

Mandy opened her mouth to say something but there was a screeching sound as somebody turned on a microphone and Mrs. Ponsonby's voice split the air.

"Ouch!" said James. "Mrs. Ponsonby doesn't need a microphone."

Mandy turned to where Mrs. Ponsonby was standing, perched on the platform with the turrets.

"And I hope you will all have a wonderful time," Mrs. Ponsonby was saying. "Don't forget to spend lots of money at the booths. Remember, it's for a good cause."

Mandy suddenly caught sight of a woman in a long black gown with a white veil walking toward them. She was with a man on crutches.

"Look!" she said to James. "There's Mr. Hurst. But who's that with him?"

James screwed up his eyes and shoved his glasses up on his nose.

"It's the head nurse," he said. "She's dressed as a medieval nun. She looks great!"

"Hi, Mr. Hurst!" Mandy called. "It's great to see you out of the hospital."

"It's great to *be* out of the hospital," Mr. Hurst said, stopping beside them. Then he turned to the nurse. "Not that I'm complaining about the care I had," he said.

The head nurse smiled. "I understand perfectly," she said. "I'm always glad to see my patients go home, too."

Mandy looked around for Polly, but Mrs. Ponsonby's voice caught her attention.

"I'm sure you've all heard the story of what happened at the bridge by now," she said. "And as you know, the Lady of the Manor always presents her favor to the bravest knight. But I want to present my favor to the bravest *pony* — and the smartest."

As Mandy watched, Susan rode out in front of the platform, followed by Polly on Shona. Susan held back as Polly walked Shona right up to the edge of the plat-

form. Mrs. Ponsonby took the huge red ribbon from her
bodice and bent over to pin it to Shona's bridle.

Mandy looked at Mr. Hurst, standing beside the head
nurse. His mouth was open, as if he couldn't believe his
eyes. Then the nurse guided him toward the front of the
crowd and Polly turned Shona to face them. The little
girl caught sight of her father and her face lit up. She
touched her heels to Shona's flanks and began to walk
the Shetland pony toward him.

"Daddy!" she said, her eyes sparkling. "Did you see? Did you see Shona getting her prize?"

Mr. Hurst reached up and Polly tumbled into his arms. "I saw," he said to her. "And I've never been more proud in my life."

Mandy moved forward to take Shona's bridle as Polly clung to her father as if she would never let him go.

Mr. Hurst looked over the top of Polly's head at Mandy as she gathered Shona's reins in her hand. "Something tells me you had a lot to do with this," he said.

Mandy blushed but luckily she didn't have to say anything. There was a screech from the platform.

Mrs. Ponsonby clutched at her head just as a gust of wind caught her hennin. It lifted off her head and flew upward, the veil beating the air like wings. Then it floated down to the other end of the field.

"Well, she did say it was supposed to be a butterfly," said Mandy.

James looked at Blackie. "Fetch, boy!" he said.

Blackie went streaking off after the hennin while Mrs. Ponsonby clutched at her hair. Blackie gently picked up the hennin in his mouth and began to trot back across the field with it.

"Amazing!" said Mandy, looking pointedly at James's sweatpants. "He doesn't seem to have torn the veil at all."

James coughed. "Mmm," he said. "Pity about the tights."

Mandy looked from James's sweatpants to Polly and her dad. Mr. Hurst had an arm around his daughter, giving her the biggest hug, and Polly's face was shining with pleasure. Shona stood patiently beside Mandy, nibbling grass. Mandy grinned.

So James hadn't worn the tights, she thought. *You can't win them all!*